MARVEL CINEMATIC UNIVERSE
PHASE ONE

MARVEL

THOR

MARVEL CINEMATIC UNIVERSE
PHASE ONE

MARVEL

THOR

Adapted by **ALEX IRVINE**

Based on the Screenplay by
ASHLEY EDWARD MILLER & ZACK STENTZ and **DON PAYNE**

Produced by **KEVIN FEIGE**

Directed by **KENNETH BRANAGH**

LITTLE, BROWN AND COMPANY
New York   Boston

marvelkids.com

© 2015 MARVEL

Little, Brown and Company

Hachette Book Group
1290 Avenue of the Americas, New York, NY 10104
Visit us at lb-kids.com

Little, Brown and Company is a division of Hachette Book Group, Inc. The Little, Brown name and logo are trademarks of Hachette Book Group, Inc.

The publisher is not responsible for websites (or their content) that are not owned by the publisher.

First Edition: January 2015

Library of Congress Cataloging-in-Publication Data

Irvine, Alexander (Alexander C.)
Phase one : Thor / adapted by Alex Irvine ; based on the screenplay by Ashley Edward Miller and Zack Stentz and Don Payne.—First edition.
pages cm.—(Marvel cinematic universe)
ISBN 978-0-316-25635-3 (hardcover)—ISBN 978-0-316-38356-1 (ebook)—ISBN 978-0-316-38358-5 (library edition ebook) 1. Graphic novels. I. Thor (Motion picture) II. Title.
PZ7.7.I78Php 2015
741.5'973—dc23
2014037861

10 9 8 7 6 5 4 3 2 1

RRD-C

Printed in the United States of America

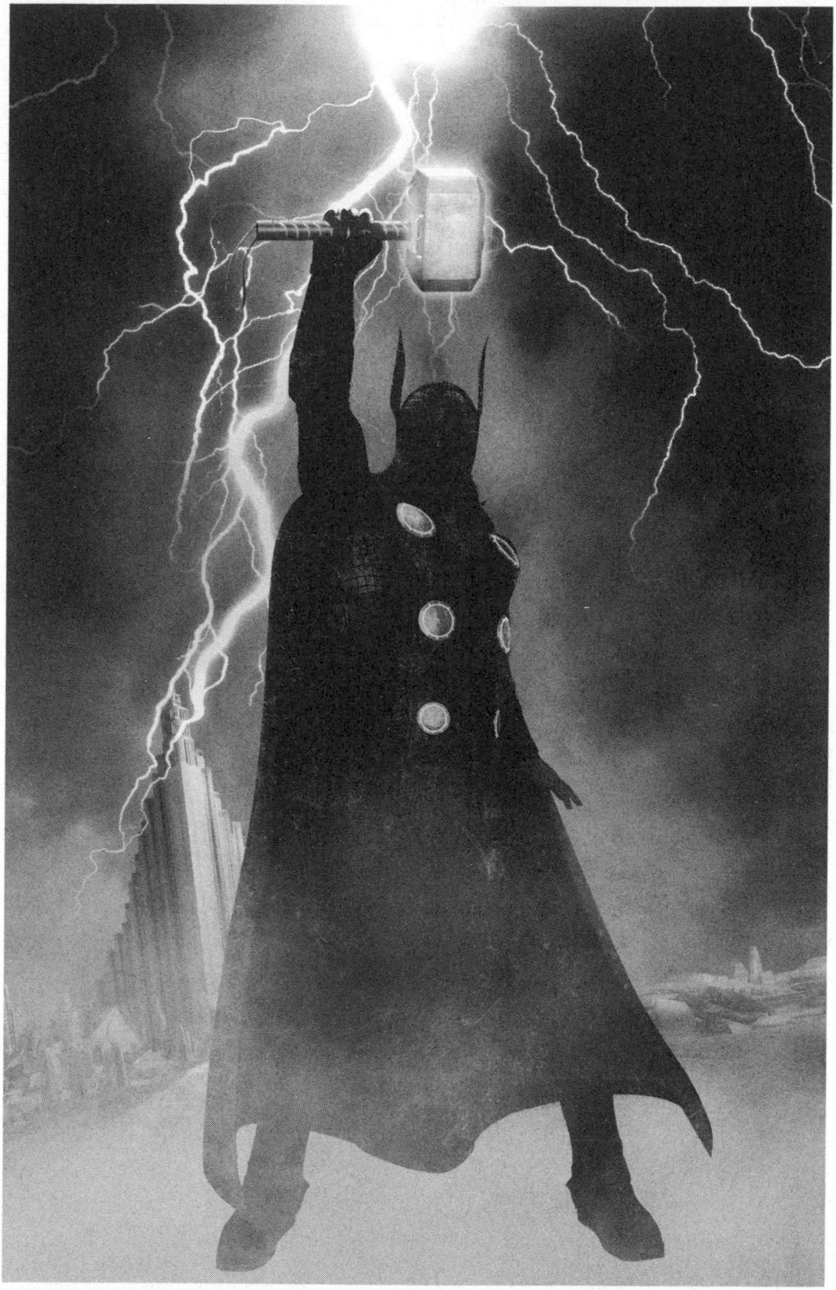

PROLOGUE

They've always asked questions—this race called man, on this planet called Earth. Passionately longing to know how they are connected to the heavens. In ages past, they looked to us as gods, for indeed so many times we saved them from calamity. We tried to show them how their world was but one of the Nine Realms of the cosmos, linked to all others by the branches of Yggdrasil...the World Tree. Nine Realms in a universe of wonder, beauty, and terror that they barely comprehended.

But for all their thirst for knowledge, they let our knowledge—they let our lessons—fall into myth and dream.

The mighty Thor. Where did he—the one whom the humans call the God of Thunder—come from? He came from us, the proudest warriors the worlds have ever seen. He came from this—the greatest realm the universe has ever known.

Thor came from Asgard.

And these are his tales....

THE ALL-FATHER'S FEAR

The All-Father did not act without thought. Now, as the sun shone over Asgard and the buildings were illuminated by its rays, gleaming like gold, he thought long and hard. At the realm's edge, the darkness of the cosmos spread out like a calm sea. Asgard was at peace, and all was ready for the momentous events to come.

Standing in his chambers, Odin stared out at the realm he had ruled for so many years. Despite the beauty before him, his mind was troubled and his expression drawn with worry and tension.

As All-Father, Odin had battled great beasts, invaded foreign realms, destroyed strong enemies, and kept the realm of Asgard safe and peaceful. He had lost his brothers and father to war. For thousands upon thousands of years, he had carried the burden of his crown alone. It had wearied him at times, energized him at others. When he had married his wife, Frigga, the burden had lifted, as she was a strong partner and had a helpful ear. And with the birth of his first son, Thor, Odin had felt hopeful that one day he would be able to pass along his crown to a worthy successor and find the peace he so rightly deserved.

Now that day had finally come. For today, Thor would become king.

Yet Odin did not feel a sense of relief.

With a deep sigh, he turned from the wide doorway that led out to his chamber balcony. Behind him, the two giant statues of his fallen brothers standing outside the palace framed his tired body, dwarfing him, while at the same time hinting at his great might and heritage. He was not yet dressed for the evening, still in the golden robes that he would soon exchange for his ceremonial gear. But his hair was combed and his face freshly shaved. Odin's shoulder-length hair was no longer the blond of his youth, but the gray suited him and he still had the bearing of a great warrior and powerful leader.

Queen Frigga sat at her vanity, putting on her jewelry. In the reflection, she saw her husband turn and come back into the center of the room. His blue eyes were dark with worry, and she felt a now long-familiar rush of love. She had married a warrior, but knew him as so much more than that. He did not rule lightly. Everything he had done and everything he would do was the result of great reflection. He had seen the results of battles that had not been thought out and had lost too many warriors to unnecessary violence. And so she knew that he had thought long and hard about this day.

While some argued that Thor should have assumed the throne years ago, Odin had seen the benefit in waiting. He wanted his son to follow in his footsteps and the footsteps of his father before him—to keep Asgard safe and free of war. Yet Thor was not his father. Thor was impulsive and hotheaded. He still had much to learn about the value of patience. Alas, Odin had no more time left to teach. He was growing weaker by the day. Soon, he would need to enter the Odinsleep, during which he would be unable to rule, his body in a state of suspended animation while he used the powerful Odinforce to rejuvenate.

Feeling his wife's gaze on him, Odin looked up and smiled, the corners of his eyes crinkling. She continued to amaze him. Her beauty was beyond compare, and while servants rushed about in preparation below, she sat calmly, her back straight and her head high. Now, more than ever, he needed her strength.

"Do you think he's ready?" Odin asked, his voice deep with emotion.

She looked at him and nodded slowly. "Thor has his father's wisdom," she said, knowing that was what he needed to hear. But Odin's expression remained worried, so she added, "He won't be alone. Loki will be at his side to give him counsel."

She stood up and approached her husband. Loki,

their younger son, was a source of tension between them. Odin had always favored Thor because Thor was a warrior, just like him, but Loki was not, and so his younger had formed a closer bond with Queen Frigga. But in a way, that had been a good balance. Loki was Thor's opposite—quiet, thoughtful, and content to stay in the shadows. Frigga hoped that Odin would see the benefit of having the brothers side by side.

He reached out a hand, about to caress her cheek. But he stopped suddenly.

Odin's hand was shaking. The All-Father stood staring at it with fierce concentration, as though willing it to stop. "If only we had more time," Odin said when his hand finally stopped shaking. "I can fight it a little longer...."

Frigga held up a hand. "No! You've put it off too long!" she said harshly. Then her expression softened. "I worry for you."

Odin cocked his head, a playful smile tugging at his lips. "I've destroyed demons and monsters, devastated whole worlds, laid waste to mighty kingdoms, and still you worry for me?"

"Always," Frigga answered truthfully. She knew what he was capable of, but she still feared that Thor's new role would be Odin's undoing.

But she didn't have to worry. Her words had reassured her husband as they always did, and now, for better or worse, he was ready to pass the throne on to his elder son.

In a few short minutes, the mighty Thor would succeed his father and become the new king of Asgard. All attention would be on him, just as he liked it. No one would notice Thor's younger brother. No one would notice Loki the Trickster. And that's just the way Loki liked it.

Loki paused behind thick curtains as he made his way toward the elaborate throne room. For now it was quiet, with no sign of the large crowds of Asgardians who would soon fill the space. It was just Loki. On his head he wore his great helmet, its two horns rising up and then curving like a ram's. He was dressed in his finest clothes and wore his signature green cape. He soaked in the silence and for a moment, imagined that it was he who would walk down the aisle to kneel in front of

Odin and ascend to the throne of Asgard. He imagined thunderous applause and saw his mother glowing with pride as he stood, ready to rule.

Hearing the sound of loud footsteps, he shook off the fantasy and turned. His brother was striding down the long hall toward him. Towering over even the tallest of Asgardians, his chest broad and his shoulders straight, Thor held Mjolnir in his hand as he walked, and his long red cape flowed out behind him. Even Thor's helmet seemed more powerful than Loki's, its wings catching rays of sun and looking perfect atop his golden locks.

"Nervous, brother?" Loki said when Thor came to a stop in front of him. His eyes were teasing. He knew that Thor never got nervous.

"How do I look?" Thor asked, ignoring his brother's question. He adjusted his red cape and ran a hand over his armor. He may not have been nervous, but he did want to make sure that he looked the part. He had been waiting for this day for years. Nothing could spoil it for him now.

"Like a king," Loki answered, his eyes flashing.

Thor gave him a quizzical look. Loki's answer had been honest, but his tone had held a hint of something he couldn't quite read. Jealousy? Anger? Envy? His younger brother had always been something of a mystery to him. While Thor had been eager to spread his wings, fight in battles, and go off on grand adventures, Loki had always been more hesitant. True, he had Thor's back, but it was often only out of necessity. So why would Loki be jealous now? He couldn't want the throne for himself, could he?

As if sensing Thor's hesitation, Loki smiled, erasing the fire in his eyes and replacing it with affection. Then, to Thor's amusement, he turned to a servant passing by with a goblet full of wine. The wine morphed into a swarm of writhing eels that slithered up the servant's hand and arm. The servant let out a scream and dropped the goblet, which clattered to the ground. Instantly, the eels disappeared and were replaced by spilled wine. Thor laughed, reassured. Loki was a trickster and a magician. He did not want to be king.

Then Loki spoke, confirming Thor's thoughts. "I've looked forward to this day as long as you have," he said, his voice serious. "You're my brother and my friend. Sometimes I'm envious, but never doubt I love you."

Suddenly, a horn blasted. It was time for the ceremony to begin.

Inside the throne room, Asgardians had gathered to bid farewell to their current king and welcome their new one. Ceremonial banners fluttered from the high ceilings while attendants handed out golden goblets full of sweet drinks to the beautifully dressed guests. There was a festive air to the room as people chatted softly to each other and waited with eager anticipation for the arrival of the royal family.

At the front of the room, Thor's best friends and fellow warriors, Volstagg, Fandral, Hogun, and Lady Sif, stood at attention while members of the palace guard lined up in formation. Then Frigga entered the room and walked down the long aisle, Loki by her side. Her hair cascaded over her shoulders and down her back in ringlets that matched her golden gown. When they had made their way to the front of the room, another horn sounded, and the guards stepped aside. There was an audible gasp.

Odin sat atop his golden throne. On his head he wore a large helmet, and in his hand he gripped the mighty spear Gungnir.

Looking out over the room, Odin sighed deeply. Even after ruling for tens of thousands of years, he felt as if it were only a day ago that his father had crowned him in a ceremony similar to this one. He wondered now if his father had had the same doubts about him that he was having about Thor. *Did he regret having to step aside for the younger generation to take over?* Odin thought. *Was I as impulsive then as Thor is now? Does that mean that he, too, will grow into a wise king in time?*

Odin's thoughts were interrupted by another gasp from the crowd. Then the room erupted in applause. The mighty Thor had arrived.

Thor raised Mjolnir, the hammer that only the worthy could lift, high over his head and soaked in the adoration. His body was covered in battle armor with large metal disks on the front chest plate. His winged helmet sat on his head, and his long red cape flowed behind him. While moments ago, everyone had believed Odin to be the most powerful ruler they would ever have, the appearance of Thor made them believe otherwise. Standing there, he looked every inch a king.

When the cheering faded, Thor finally strode up the long aisle, a smug smile on his face. Clearly the concerns of his father did not trouble Thor. He felt more than ready to rule Asgard. He had watched his father do it for years, and he thought it was time for a fresh start. He had proven himself to be one of the finest warriors the realm had ever seen. Now he would prove himself to be one of its finest kings.

As Odin watched his son walk toward him, the gravity of the situation hit the All-Father hard. Though sometimes brash and irresponsible, Thor had grown into a fine young man. And now he was about to take the throne as the new ruler of Asgard. Odin could still vividly remember when Thor was just a boy, learning how to hold a sword for the first time. Or when he was first able to wield Mjolnir. How the hammer, which now looked small in his large hands, had nearly toppled Thor!

Odin smiled now, thinking back on that day. Learning to be king would be like learning to ride a horse. Thor wouldn't like having to go slowly, and he would fall a few times, but his difficulties would serve to teach him some valuable lessons. Or so Odin hoped. He could be only grateful that the realm was at peace and had been for a long time. There was no doubt Thor was a good warrior—but a warrior king? That was another story. That was something he had yet to learn.

Finally, Thor arrived in front of his father. He nodded at his mother and brother and friends and then knelt, bowed his head, and waited. A hush fell over the crowd as they, too, waited.

"A new day has come for a new king to wield his own weapon," Odin began, his deep voice echoing through the room. "Today, I entrust you with the sacred throne of Asgard. Responsibility, duty, honor. They are essential to every soldier and every king." As the All-Father spoke, Thor raised his eyes to look at him. Odin willed the words to impact his son, to get through to him. For after this day, he would be on his own.

Odin continued, repeating the declaration that had been spoken to him so many years before. He was at the very end of his speech when he felt it—a chill that cut through the room and caused people to shiver uncertainly. Odin's heart began to race. He had felt this chill before—on Jotunheim. Asgard had waged a long and fierce war with the ice realm. But a truce had been made years ago. There was no reason for Odin to think Jotuns would be in Asgard. Still . . .

Shaking off the feeling of dread, Odin continued. He was just about to say the final words that would make Thor king when the banners hanging from the ceiling suddenly iced over.

There was no denying it. "Frost Giants," Odin whispered.

A GROWING CHILL

After leaving so Thor could prepare for his entrance, Loki had made his way to the front of the throne room. The Warriors Three—Volstagg, Fandral, and Hogun—were already at their places of honor, along with Lady Sif. The four were Thor's lifelong friends. Together, they had gone on many adventures in which Loki had taken only a reluctant part.

The room had grown crowded and was filled with muffled conversation as everybody eagerly awaited

Thor's arrival. But first, Odin appeared, seated on his golden throne, spear in hand. His expression showed pride—and perhaps a hint of sadness—as he looked out over the room. Loki felt a pang, wondering if Odin had ever looked that way at him. Shaking off the thought, he focused on the door again.

"Where is he?" Loki heard Volstagg mutter. "I'm famished. And Odin will not be happy with the delay."

Turning, Loki gave him a look. The huge warrior was always hungry. "I wouldn't worry," he said softly. "Father will forgive him. He always does."

Then, as if in response to Loki's words, the room erupted in applause. Standing at the opposite end of the throne room holding his hammer high above his head was Loki's brother and the future king of Asgard, the mighty Thor.

As Thor knelt in front of Odin, Loki watched, his expression unreadable. Today, everything would change. For better or worse, he could not tell. Would Thor be a good king? A wise king? Or would he be a rash and foolish one? There were times Loki doubted that Thor was ready—he didn't listen and he was quick to judge. Would Asgard benefit from such a leader? Watching him now, as Odin spoke the words his own father had spoken to him thousands of years before, Loki had to admit Thor looked like a king.

Odin had just gotten to the final part of the ceremony when a chill filled the room. Loki shivered and rubbed his arms. Trying to ignore the feeling, Loki turned his attention back to Odin, who hadn't stopped. But then, the banners that hung from the high ceilings suddenly crackled.

Upon his throne, Odin's expression grew serious. He seemed to know exactly what was causing this strange phenomenon. "Frost Giants," Loki heard him hiss.

And then, as he and everyone else watched in shock, Thor stood up and ran from the room. The Warriors Three and Lady Sif followed. Sighing, Odin went after them.

Loki turned and looked at his mother. "What is going on?" he asked.

"I have no idea," Frigga answered. "But I suggest you go and find out."

Odin ordered the guards to be on alert and then followed the chill out of the room. Thor was ahead of him, charging down toward the Vault, the deep labyrinth where Asgard's greatest treasures and direst threats were held...under the protection of the Destroyer. He had a very good idea about what the Frost Giants were after—the Casket of Ancient Winters. The Casket enabled anyone who held it to create a never-ending winter. Laufey, the Jotun king, had wanted to use the Casket to turn all the realms into frozen ice lands that he could rule. Years earlier, Odin had taken the Casket in order to ensure it would never be misused. For the safety of all Nine Realms, he had it placed in the Vault. Although it was guarded at all times, someone must have gotten in.

When he arrived at the Vault, his assumptions were proven true. He found Thor, with Sif and the Warriors Three, staring at the remains of a great battle. Two Asgardian sentries lay on the floor, frozen solid.

Towering above them stood the Destroyer, Odin's deadliest weapon. It was a suit of armor, three times the size of a man, animated by the mystical Odinforce. When a threat to Odin or Asgard was felt, the Destroyer would awaken, and the Odinforce would burn bright, laying waste to anyone or anything that got in its way. The Jotuns who had found their way into the Vault had not survived to find their way out.

Now, the Destroyer held the Casket of Ancient Winters in its hands.

Thor turned, and his eyes met his father's. While Odin's eyes were troubled and resigned, Thor's blazed with unabashed fury. This was an act of war! While up above, a roomful of the most important people in the Nine Realms had been celebrating, the Vault had been broken into and two sentries killed. All of Asgard could be at risk. Something had to be done.

Odin watched as various emotions played over his son's face. He knew Thor was angry and that he wanted revenge. A part of him wanted that, too. If Laufey had sent the Frost Giants, it meant that he no longer valued the truce. On the other hand, if Laufey hadn't sent them, and the rogue Jotuns had acted on their own, then Odin might be starting an unnecessary war by retaliating. To Odin, the more troubling question was how the Jotuns had gotten into Asgard. With the all-seeing Heimdall stationed at the base of the Bifrost—the Rainbow Bridge connecting the Nine Realms—it should have been impossible for anyone to enter unnoticed.

"The Jotuns must pay for what they've done!" Thor shouted, interrupting his father's thoughts.

"They have paid," Odin said softly. "The ultimate price."

Thor didn't care. He was burning with the desire to avenge this insult to Asgard. "This is an act of war!"

The king shook his head sadly. He had hoped Thor would think rationally about the consequences. "I have a truce with Laufey," Odin reminded Thor.

"He just broke your truce," Thor said. "We must act!"

Odin turned to Thor's friends. "Leave us," he

commanded. When he was alone with his son, he asked, "What action would you take?"

Thor puffed out his chest. He knew exactly what he would do. "March into Jotunheim as you once did and teach them a lesson."

"The Casket of Ancient Winters belonged to the Jotuns. They believe it's their birthright," Odin said, his voice heavy.

"And if they had it, they would lay waste to the Nine Realms!"

"This was the action of but a few, doomed to fail," Odin said. "We will find the breach in our defenses, and it will be sealed."

"As king of Asgard," Thor began, and Odin lost his patience.

"But you're not king yet!" he roared. Father and son stared each other down for a long moment. Odin knew Thor thought him weak, but Odin had the well-being of Asgard to consider. Thor thought only as a warrior. Under no circumstances would Odin permit Thor to travel to Jotunheim. It would solve nothing and most certainly send the realms into war. Thor was not ready for such a war, and Odin feared he was too old to see it through.

Thor looked as though he might challenge his father. His face was hard and his eyes glittered with anger. But without saying anything, he turned on his heel and left the Vault.

Alone with the dead sentries and the bodies of the Jotun warriors, Odin felt his limbs begin to shake. He was uneasy and unsure about Asgard's future and about his own health—and that frightened him.

Thor stood in the banquet hall, stewing over the argument with his father. No, he was not king yet; but it was his birthright, and he was not going to let a few words in a ceremony stand between him and protecting Asgard. His brother and his friends were there, unsure how to speak to him in the midst of his rage.

Finally, it was Loki who took the first step toward Thor.

"If it's any consolation, I think you're right," he said.

"About the Frost Giants, about Laufey, everything. If a few of them could penetrate the defenses of Asgard once, who's to say they won't try again? Next time with an army?"

"Yes, exactly!" Thor said. He was glad his brother agreed.

"But there's nothing we can do without defying Father," Loki pointed out.

Thor considered this. He looked out the banquet hall window over the splendor of Asgard. Then he looked down at Mjolnir. Loki saw Thor get a gleam in his eye. The kind of gleam he got when he saw a chance for battle.

"No," Loki said. "Stop there! I know that look!"

"It's the only way to ensure the safety of our borders," Thor said. "We're going to Jotunheim."

Fandral was usually up for anything Thor proposed, but this idea stunned him. "What!?"

Sif was more serious. "Thor, of all the laws of Asgard, this is one you must not break."

"If the Frost Giants don't kill you, your father will!" Volstagg added.

Thor didn't care. He knew this was the right thing to do. "My father fought his way into Jotunheim, defeated their armies, and took their Casket! We'd just be looking for answers."

"It is forbidden!" Sif warned.

Thor spread his arms and brought his brother and his friends close to him. "My friends, trust me now. We must do this."

There was a pause. Then Loki said, "Yes, of course! I won't let my brother march into Jotunheim alone. I will be at his side."

"And I," Volstagg said.

Fandral nodded. "And I."

Hogun, a warrior of few words, nodded as well. "The Warriors Three fight together."

"I fear we'll live to regret this," Sif said.

Volstagg rolled his eyes. "If we're lucky."

All they had to do was get past Heimdall, the guardian of the Bifrost. He had the gift of seeing anything that happened anywhere in the Nine Realms. He would certainly be ready for them. As the watcher over the Bifrost, he was sworn to be loyal to Odin; if the All-Father had forbidden travel to Jotunheim, Heimdall would prevent Thor and his friends from making the journey.

But Thor had to ask.

Loki wanted to take the lead and convince Heimdall to permit their voyage, but Thor had no patience to wait. When they reached the gateway to the Observatory, where Heimdall stood his endless watch, Thor strode forward.

"Heimdall, may we pass?" he asked.

For a long moment Heimdall just stared at them from under his heavy golden helmet. When he spoke, his words were slow and careful.

"For ages have I guarded Asgard and kept it safe from those who would do it harm," he said. "In all that time, never has an enemy slipped by my watch—until this day. I wish to know how that happened."

Thor nodded. This was good news. Heimdall would let them pass even though it was against Odin's rules. "Then tell no one where we've gone until we've returned," Thor said.

Thor walked past Heimdall. The rest of the group followed. Loki looked irritated that he hadn't gotten his chance to speak. Volstagg couldn't resist needling him a little.

"What happened?" Volstagg joked. "Your silver tongue turn to lead?"

"Get me off this bridge before it cracks under your girth," Loki snapped.

Volstagg and Fandral laughed.

"Be warned," Heimdall said as the group passed him. "I will honor my sworn oath to protect this Realm as its gatekeeper. If your return threatens the safety of Asgard, Bifrost will remain closed to you." He let them think about that for a moment.

If the Bifrost did not open to them, they would be stuck in Jotunheim, surrounded by a huge army of angry Jotuns. The thought sobered them all.

Except Thor. "I have no plans to die today," he said.

Heimdall did not smile. "None do," he said.

Heimdall inserted his sword into the lock that

controlled the Bifrost, opening and closing the pathways to the Nine Realms. The great Observatory, a clockworks sphere that channeled the energies of the Bifrost, began to spin.

"All is ready," Heimdall said. "You may pass."

Thor, Loki, Sif, and the Warriors Three stepped up onto the platform at the center of the Observatory. Soon the Bifrost would appear there, allowing them to travel instantly to any of the Nine Realms.

On the outside of the Observatory was a long, narrow cone. It turned and aimed toward Jotunheim. A beam of rainbow energy shot out from it across space and became the Rainbow Bridge.

"Couldn't you just leave the bridge open for us?" Volstagg asked. He looked nervous. He always was before a possible fight.

"To keep this bridge open would unleash the full power of the Bifrost and destroy Jotunheim," Heimdall said.

The Bifrost could remain open only long enough for a group to go across it. Its energies were too powerful to contain if it stayed open for too long.

"Ah. Never mind, then," Volstagg said.

Thor started toward the Bifrost. At the edge of the bridge, he stopped and looked back toward his friends, grinning.

"Come on!" he said. "Don't be bashful."

WHAT LOKI
SAW

Loki watched all that happened in Asgard. He might not have had Heimdall's gift, but he knew what happened in this realm. He saw and heard many things that others did not, and he made his own plans. He could watch unobserved because he was the second son, the forgotten son. All eyes in Asgard followed Thor. Loki also heard and saw things a little differently than other Asgardians, because it was a gift of his to alter the way others perceived the world. Call it illusion, call it persuasion; either way, the result was that Loki made sure he always possessed information other Asgardians did not. This was his true power, just as Thor's true power lay in his limitless courage and strength.

He considered everything that had happened since the discovery of the Jotun attempt to capture the Casket of Winters. Odin had been clear: Thor was not to act upon the Jotuns. But Loki knew that his brother would not accept that command. Thor was not one to wait patiently, as he made clear by raging through the banquet hall before Loki and the Warriors Three could calm him.

His brother was pacing up and down, his long strides echoing like thunder off the walls. The Warriors Three and Lady Sif had just entered the room, their faces worried, when suddenly Thor walked over to the long table that had been set for his celebration dinner. He flipped it over as though it weighed no more than a feather. Food and drink went flying and dishes clattered to the ground and glasses shattered.

The room grew silent.

"All this food," Volstagg said, eyeing the remains of a large cake. "So innocent. Cast to the ground. It breaks the heart."

Thor shot him a look so cold that Volstagg took a step back as if he had been hit. Glancing around the room, Volstagg's gaze fell on Loki. He nodded at Loki as if to say, *Can you please do something about your wild brother?*

Loki doubted there was anything he could say or do. His powers of persuasion were known throughout Asgard, but Thor knew him well enough to know when Loki was trying to talk him into something. Even so, he felt he ought to try. He walked over, reaching out a hand to comfort Thor.

"It's unwise to be in my company right now, brother," Thor said.

Already Loki had seen the light in Thor's eyes. He knew that look. It meant Thor would not be satisfied without a battle. This was not good. Not good at all. While Thor might have been willing to risk the wrath of the king, Loki wasn't so eager to do so. He had spent too many years trying to get his father's attention, and he didn't want what attention he finally did get to come from a foolish idea of Thor's. His brother's next words confirmed his fears.

"We're going to Jotunheim," Thor stated.

"It's madness!" Loki cried, catching the attention of the others, who had been standing apart from the brothers.

"What's madness?" Volstagg asked.

"Nothing!" Loki answered, shooting his brother a look. "Thor was making a jest."

"The safety of our realm is no jest," Thor said, walking over to his fellow warriors and filling them in on his plan. "We're going to Jotunheim."

As Thor tried to convince the others, Loki moved to the side and listened. Why did he always seem to get into trouble because of his older brother? Wasn't he supposed to be the wiser one? Odin had expressly forbidden that they enter Jotunheim. Yet it wasn't the first time Thor had done something reckless. And it wouldn't be the first time Loki was powerless to stop him. Anger shot through him. Did Thor not realize what could happen if they were caught? Or worse, if they did go to Jotunheim and were overwhelmed by the Frost Giants? They would be realms away. Who would save them?

Loki had already set his own plans in motion to save Asgard from the threat of the Jotuns. He could not have Thor ruining them. Perhaps he ought to make use of his other gift—the power of illusion, to make people see what was not there and blind them to what was?

Not yet, he thought. Not yet.

Sighing, he tuned back into the conversation to hear Thor say, "My friends, trust me now. We must do this." Then he turned to Loki and raised an eyebrow as if to say, *You are in, are you not, little brother?*

There was no choice. "I won't let my brother march into Jotunheim alone," he said simply.

Loki had made a decision. True, he could not dictate his brother's actions, but that didn't mean he couldn't continue to make plans of his own. As the others checked and double-checked that they had everything they would need for their journey to Jotunheim, Loki slipped away.

When Loki rejoined the others, they were on their way to the Observatory. Hogun gave him a curious glance, but he ignored it. What he had done was none of their business.

"We must first find a way to get past Heimdall," Thor said.

"That will be no easy task," Volstagg observed, trying to get his bulky body comfortable atop his horse. "It's said the gatekeeper can see a single dewdrop fall from a blade of grass a thousand miles away."

Loki tried not to roll his eyes. Heimdall was not nearly as powerful as Volstagg claimed. He couldn't be, or else how had the Jotuns managed to sneak past him? It would take a person with true power to make that happen. That was the type of person Volstagg should fear.

Fandral seemed to agree with Loki's thoughts. "And he can hear a cricket passing gas in Niflheim," he said, his voice teasing.

"Forgive him!" Volstagg cried, raising his eyes to the sky. "He meaneth no offense!"

The others were still laughing at the big man's even bigger superstitions...except Thor, who took no notice. Loki's brother was single-minded. All he could think of was teaching the Jotuns a lesson. Within moments, they were through the tall gate that surrounded the royal city. The Observatory loomed before them. Behind it, the dark cosmos spread out, a black sea of twinkling lights, which made the domed building seem to float in the sky.

When they arrived, Heimdall was waiting for them.

"Leave this to me," Loki said, eyeing the intimidating man whose face was nearly hidden behind a gold helmet. "Good Heimdall—" Loki began to say.

The watcher over the Bifrost held up a hand, silencing him. "You think you can deceive me?" he asked, and Loki took an involuntary step backward. How much did Heimdall know? He opened his mouth to protest, but the guard went on. "I, who can sense the flapping of a butterfly's wings across the cosmos?"

Volstagg eyed the others knowingly. Turning to Loki, he teased, "Silver tongue turn to lead?"

Loki glared at him. "Get me off this bridge before it cracks under your girth," he retorted.

Once again, Heimdall held up a hand to silence them. "You are not dressed warmly enough," he said, causing Loki to breathe a sigh of relief. So that was what Heimdall knew—that they were going to attack the icy realm of Jotunheim. Heimdall must have heard about the attack in the Vault and was anxious to figure out how the giants had slipped past them.

With a nod, the group followed Heimdall to the Observatory. Loki looked up and around at the large domed ceiling, its sides covered with carvings and glittering with an unnatural bronze light. As they all looked on, Heimdall walked over to what appeared to be a large control panel in the middle of the room. He lifted up his sword and plunged it deep into the device. The room suddenly filled with a pulsating, vibrating energy—the Bifrost. Turning, Loki saw a large opening on the side of the Observatory. Beyond it, the cosmos spread out.

Heimdall plunged his sword even deeper into the device, and the Bifrost energy quickened, coalescing into a vortex of spinning rainbow light. It shot out into the darkness, creating a link with Jotunheim.

"All is ready," Heimdall said. "You may pass."

Loki hated Bifrost travel. The way the portal sucked and pulled you apart until you feared you would not recover; the shock and cold as you were sucked between realms; and the knowledge that when the Bifrost closed behind you, it might not ever open again, trapping you far from home. Still, he had no choice. The plan was in motion, and this trip was part of it.

As Thor stepped up and disappeared into the vortex, Loki paused and looked back over his shoulder as if he could see into the palace.

Turning back, he walked up to the portal entrance and took a deep breath.

One more step and he would be sucked into the swirling rainbow.

They were on their way to Jotunheim.

And what would happen once they got there was not in the hands of fate, but in the hands of his impulsive brother and his warrior friends. Loki would not be able to manipulate events there. He had to trust that the arrangements he had made would be enough for them all to survive.

THE POWER OF THREE

Volstagg had never been this cold in his entire life. Or hungry. It wasn't natural for one not to feel one's nose or lips or hands or even eyeballs. And it certainly wasn't natural for him to hear his stomach grumbling over the sound of the wind howling. No, it was entirely wrong. As was this godforsaken journey to Jotunheim that he and his fellow warriors had been talked into by Thor Odinson.

Usually, Volstagg would be up for any adventure.

His giant size was matched only by his equally large appetite for food—and excitement. And he had been at Thor's side on many a journey. It was his rightful place as a member of the Warriors Three. He, Fandral the Dashing (who, in Volstagg's opinion, was a bit too attached to mirrors and his own reflection), and Hogun the Grim (who was certainly grim, you couldn't argue with that) were famous throughout the Nine Realms. Poems had been written about the mighty band of adventurers in Nornheim. Songs had been sung of their trips to Midgard, and tales had been told of their many conquests—of both lands outside the realm and women. And they were all true—well, most of them. At least the ones that other people told. Volstagg himself believed that a bit of embellishment could go a long way.

But, unfortunately, he was not embellishing now. It *was* cold. And he did not want to be in Jotunheim.

Lifting his head slightly, Volstagg felt the sting of ice against his cheeks. He did his best to glare at Thor, who walked ahead of him, seemingly unaffected by the temperature. Volstagg tried to raise an eyebrow but his eyebrows were frozen, so he fumed instead. They shouldn't be here. Odin All-Father had expressly forbidden his son from traveling to Jotunheim. But Thor did not take kindly to orders. And he certainly didn't take kindly to having his home invaded. Which the Jotuns had done—on the very day Thor was to become the new king of Asgard.

Jotunheim had slowly decayed until it was now nothing but a world of melting and cracking ice populated by angry and bitter Frost Giants. Still, their king was strong, and Asgard could not chance starting a war with them. That was why Odin had forbidden Thor from trying to take revenge, even if he didn't like it that his realm had been invaded. They couldn't risk a war.

Thor had raged, furious about being kept on a tight leash. If the day had gone according to plan, he would have been made king. And as king, he would have been the one making decisions.

Volstagg could have predicted what happened next: Thor had turned on the charm to get the Warriors Three to help him.

"My friends," he had said to the Warriors Three, Lady Sif, and Loki when the group had gathered in one of the great banquet halls, "have you forgotten all that we've done together?"

Thor turned to Hogun, undaunted by his grim expression and crossed arms. Thor was used to seeing the silent man with a scowl on his handsome face. While others quaked at the sight of the warrior who always had his large spiked mace by his side, Thor was never daunted—even on the occasions when he should be. Such as now. Still, he went on: "Who led you into the most glorious of battles?" he asked Hogun, who gave a measured nod in response.

Thor approached Fandral, who was relishing his own reflection. "And who led you on adventures so dangerous that female admirers and adoring fans continue to follow you around to this day?"

Fandral flashed his winning smile. "It was you, my Prince," Fandral said, proud of his exploits.

Then Thor walked over and put an arm around Volstagg. He had to reach up, as Volstagg was one of the few Asgardians taller than Thor. With his other hand, Thor patted Volstagg's large belly. "And who led you to delicacies so succulent you thought you'd died and gone to Valhalla?"

"You did," Volstagg said, his stomach growling.

Thor smiled smugly. Finally he turned to Lady Sif. She was, as always, wearing a long sword across her back, and he knew all too well that there were more weapons hidden in her armor. While she was one of the most beautiful women in all the realms, her beauty was matched by her expert sword skills. No one dared mess with her. No one except Thor. "And who proved wrong all who scoffed at the idea that a young maiden could be one of the fiercest warriors this realm has ever known?" he asked.

She raised one perfectly arched eyebrow, and the corner of her mouth lifted up in the barest hint of a smile. "I did," she said simply.

The others let out a nervous laugh as Thor nodded. "True," he admitted. "But I supported you." Then he turned back to the rest of the group. "My friends, trust me now. We must do this."

And so they did.

A piece of ice hit Volstagg in the cheek, bringing him abruptly back to the situation at hand. Once more, he cursed the Frost Giants for ever making this trip necessary.

Beside him, Fandral looked equally upset by the situation. The charming warrior hated to be anywhere he needed to cover his face. And he really did not like being far from women and a nice flagon of ale. Hogun walked a bit ahead. Volstagg couldn't tell how he was feeling, since the man looked as grim as he did on the sunniest of days on Asgard.

Thor was still irritatingly cheerful. "It feels good, doesn't it?" he shouted over his shoulder. "To be together again, adventuring on another world."

"Is that what we're doing?" Fandral called back.

"What would you call it?" Thor asked, sounding honestly perplexed.

"Freezing," Fandral replied.

"Starving," Volstagg couldn't help but add.

Silence fell over the group as they continued to trek across the frozen wasteland. *How could anything dangerous come from this realm?* Volstagg wondered as he walked. It seemed completely abandoned. Occasionally they would pass what might have been a house or small village. But the buildings had long since fallen into disrepair, and only the faintest skeleton of a frame could sometimes be seen through the ice. Volstagg felt an involuntary shiver that had nothing to do with the cold. This realm had once been one of the mightiest and most feared of Asgard's enemies. But now it seemed pitiful. Had Odin really caused such devastation? The Casket of Eternal Winters seemed a heavy price to pay, looking at the realm now. Perhaps the Frost Giants were right to want it back.

Volstagg shook off these thoughts. It was not his place to wonder. He was here to help Thor confront Laufey. And it looked as if that was about to happen. They had arrived at the central plaza of Jotunheim.

As soon as they walked into the plaza, the wind died down and the ice stopped pelting their faces. Cautiously, they took off the hoods that had been offering them a bit of protection and raised their eyes to scan their surroundings. Each warrior kept a steady hand near his weapon in case of ambush.

But they seemed to be alone. The only noise came from the walls that creaked and melted around them and also from Volstagg's labored breathing. Fandral shot him a look. "Could you keep it down?" he said. "Or would you like them to know exactly where to throw their ice spears?"

"They would just need to see your shiny hair to know where to aim," Volstagg replied. "How much time did you spend brushing back those lovely locks of yours this morning? Ten minutes? An hour?"

"Hush," Lady Sif hissed. "Both of you. I don't think we're alone anymore."

And she was right. Volstagg felt the hairs on the back of his neck rise as, out of the shadows and from behind the crumbling columns, Frost Giants appeared. Their blue skin looked as cold as the rest of the planet, and they were very, very big. Even Volstagg looked small next to them. As they stepped into the light, he noticed that each giant had a different build. One of them had a large, wide, domed forehead while another had one arm that hung longer than the other and tapered into a very narrow hand.

"What is your business here?" one of the giants hissed.

Thor took a step forward, and in a choreographed move, the giants took a step forward as well, tightening the circle around the Asgardians. "I speak only to your king," Thor said, his strong voice bouncing off the walls.

"Then speak," another voice replied from the shadows of a balcony above them.

Volstagg narrowed his eyes as he tried to make out the speaker. He caught a glimpse of a long, lean giant slowly making his way to the foreground. There was a slight stoop to his shoulders, which indicated that he might be old, but his voice was still full of pride. This must be the Frost Giant king.

As if in confirmation of Volstagg's thoughts, the giant stepped forward out of the shadows. "I am Laufey," he said, "king of this realm." His voice crackled as he spoke, like the ice that melted and broke apart all around him.

Volstagg had heard many tales of the famed king of the Frost Giants, mostly from Thor and Loki, who had heard Odin's stories growing up. He knew the king had no fear of battle. His fierce fighting style was second only to Odin's, and over the years, he'd lost many Jotuns to battles among the various realms. Seeing the king now, Volstagg could believe the stories. Despite the state of his realm, Laufey looked noble and far too proud to reveal the giants had suffered at all.

"I demand answers!" Thor called up to the king, obviously unconcerned with the giant's reputation. "How did your people get into Asgard?"

"The house of Odin is full of traitors," Laufey said cryptically.

Turning, Volstagg exchanged a confused glance with Fandral and Hogun. Traitors? What was Laufey talking about? Asgard had no traitors.

Thor apparently agreed. His grip on his hammer tightened and he took another step forward. "Do not dishonor my father's name with your lies!" he cried.

"Why have you come here?" Laufey asked rhetorically. "To make peace? No. You long for battle." From the look on the king's face, Volstagg guessed that the giant would be happy to oblige.

As if on cue, a few more Frost Giants stepped into view. This was not good.

Lady Sif seemed to feel the same way. She shot Loki a look, hoping Thor's younger brother would take the hint. He needed to say something—now.

Loki, who had been rather silent up until this point, nodded. He walked over and put a warning hand on his brother's arm. "Stop and think," he said, trying to reason with his hotheaded brother. "We are outnumbered."

Thor dragged his gaze, which had been fixed on Laufey, away from the balcony. Shaking off his brother's arm, he looked around. For the first time, he seemed to notice the Frost Giants. Perhaps his brother was right. Perhaps it would be wiser to leave now. Still…he had come here for a fight. Looking over, he eyed the Warriors Three and Lady Sif. They were all shaking their heads, and he could easily read their looks—they wanted to leave, too.

With one last glance at Laufey, Thor sighed and turned to go. Behind him, Volstagg said, "Thank Yggdrasil." Then Fandral laughed softly. *Perhaps this is what Thor's father had meant about being wise and patient,*

Volstagg thought. True, they had not taken revenge, but they hadn't caused irreconcilable damage either.

And then one of the Frost Giants spoke.

"Run back home, little princess," it said.

A few more minutes, Volstagg thought. *Why couldn't that giant have waited just a few more minutes to say something?*

Volstagg saw Thor lift his mighty hammer. Slowly, and with a heavy sigh, Volstagg drew his axe, Hogun clutched his mace, and Lady Sif pulled out her double-bladed sword. Reluctantly, Fandral reached for his sword and held it in front of him. Volstagg had to stifle a laugh as he caught his friend checking out his reflection in the blade's smooth metal. The Asgardians then formed a circle around Thor. Above all else, they would protect the prince.

It seemed the Jotuns were intent on protecting their own as well. They reached down and touched the puddles of chilled water at their feet. Instantly, the water traveled up their limbs and onto their bodies, freezing into weapons of various kinds. Volstagg saw the giant he had noticed earlier with the narrow hand. The ice froze over his lean limb, creating a sharp spear. The giant with the round head now had a mallet-shaped one, which he could ram into objects—or Asgard warriors. Another stepped in front of Fandral and created a sword and spiked armor out of the water. The ice glinted and sparkled dangerously.

"I'm hoping that's just decorative," Fandral said.

But it wasn't. The battle was on.

The sound of clashing metal and ice filled the plaza as Frost Giants and Asgardians faced off. Volstagg sighed as the mallet-headed giant raced at him. As Volstagg stepped to the side at the last moment, his aggressor ran right by him and crashed into a wall. The palace shook with the blow. "Maybe next time," Volstagg said merrily, before turning to another approaching giant. Beside him, Fandral ducked and weaved, his sword swishing through the air as he confidently dispatched giant after giant. Despite the overwhelming odds, he seemed to be having a good time.

Even Hogun looked pleased. Or, rather, at least a little less grim. Out of the corner of his eye, Volstagg watched Hogun face off against one of the giants. Hogun was clearly winning when the giant suddenly managed to back him up against one of the walls. He pulled his sword arm back, ready to strike. Hogun raised his mace high over his head, embedding it in the wall above. As the giant plunged forward, Hogun swung up and over him. Then, in midair, he pulled the mace out of the wall and landed behind the giant. With one swift move, he knocked the Jotun, now unconscious, aside.

But the Jotuns kept coming. Volstagg knew the giants needed to be stopped soon. The longer the battle continued, the worse the odds. The treacherous Frost Giants outnumbered them. To overtake them, the Asgardians would have to do something bold, something daring, something only the Warriors Three were capable of.

Fandral seemed to be on the same page as Volstagg, as he yelled out, "What move do you think?"

Volstagg stepped out of the way of an approaching Jotun and then used his giant belly to knock him over. "I say we use the Norn's Revenge," he shouted back.

"At this close range?" Fandral replied, swiping the frozen arm off one of the giants. "I think the Alfheim Lunge is a better move."

Volstagg paused. The Alfheim Lunge. It *could* work...perhaps. But it was rather embarrassing. And they had done it only that one time. Just as his mind started to drift back to that day, a blast of cold air startled Volstagg into the present.

The Alfheim Lunge, as the Warriors Three had dubbed it upon their arrival back in Asgard, was indeed a useful trick. But they were in the middle of a heated battle. It did not seem the time. Volstagg was just about to ask Fandral for another idea when Hogun rushed past him.

"Shut up!" he ordered. "And fight!"

Volstagg took an involuntary step back and had to duck as a Frost Giant swung a large block of ice at him. Hogun never spoke in battle. It was one of his rules. So if he was breaking it now, they were in far more danger than Volstagg had thought. Swinging around with his sword in hand, Volstagg sent the giant flying into a deep crevasse. Then he turned and held his weapon at the ready.

Across the way, Fandral continued to dodge and weave as he took out more Jotuns. Right outside the plaza, Lady Sif was holding her own, her shield raised and her sword swishing back and forth so fast it was almost impossible to see. Glancing behind him, Volstagg saw that Thor was busy defending himself as well. A circle of giants had formed around him as though he were in an arena and they were each waiting their turn to fight him. His hammer swung wildly, crackling with light and energy.

So far, the tide was on their side. But that could change any minute. The giants kept coming, and the Asgardians had no backup. It was going to be a difficult fight.

Turning back to the Jotuns in front of him, Volstagg let out a mighty roar and charged into the fray. No, now was not the time for the Alfheim Lunge. That was a move to use another time, in another battle.

Today, they just had to survive.

THE ALL-FATHER'S
BURDEN

din spent an uneasy night and felt no better in the morning. He had not seen Thor since their argument in the Vault. There had been shouting in the banquet hall as Thor told friends what had happened, but Odin had heard nothing since. Frigga had tried to reassure him that Thor's temper would ease and this would blow over, but Odin knew better. His son felt himself to be king already, whether the ceremony had been completed or not. He would take action. It was his nature. Odin hoped only that the action would not cause more problems than it solved.

Just then, a guard rushed over to him, and Odin's misgivings were proved correct. Thor had taken his friends and journeyed into Jotunheim. Odin felt a deep well of fury rise up within him. Thor had deliberately disobeyed his orders. So, too, had Heimdall, who should not have let anyone pass on the Bifrost—especially not a war party going to Jotunheim.

"Tell the barn master to have Sleipnir saddled and my battle gear readied immediately," he ordered the guard. It had been many years since Odin had seen the frozen realm of Jotunheim, but apparently his fate held yet one more trip to that realm. He hoped it would be in time to save Thor from his own foolishness.

Moments later, Odin raced across the Rainbow Bridge astride his eight-legged steed. Odin was right to worry. Thor—along with Loki, the Warriors Three, and Lady

Sif—had broken the truce and entered Jotunheim, thereby endangering them all.

The wind whipped Odin's face, but he didn't notice. His anger had been replaced by fear. Jotunheim was nothing but an icy wasteland now. Its surface cracked and broke apart constantly, leaving less and less of the realm. And the Frost Giants were fierce warriors with the ability to create weapons made of ice that were as sharp as the finest Asgardian blades. He did not want to think about what Thor and his band of five would be going through right now. He urged his horse to go faster.

Odin felt the familiar sense of his body being tugged and pulled out of proportion and then a sudden rush as all his molecules came crashing back together. A moment later there was a great ripping sound and a hole opened up in front of him. Beyond it he could make out the white ice of Jotunheim—and Thor. His son and the other warriors were completely surrounded by Frost Giants!

Landing, Sleipnir reared up, his powerful front legs

pawing the air. Odin's arrival stopped everyone in his or her tracks, giving Odin the chance to race over to Laufey. Odin reined Sleipnir in next to the Jotun king, and said, quietly enough that only Laufey could hear, "Laufey. End this."

"Your boy sought this out," Laufey said. He addressed Odin with respect, but no fear. They were both kings in their own realms, and Laufey feared no one.

"You're right. These are the actions of a boy," Odin said. "Treat them as such. You and I can stop this before there's further bloodshed."

Laufey sized Odin up, seeing the All-Father aged but still powerful. Odin saw the same in his Jotun counterpart. Laufey's blue skin was aged and wrinkled, but there was still pride in his stance—and strength. He shook his head. "We are beyond diplomacy now, All-Father," Laufey replied. "He'll get what he came for—war and death." Looking over at his son, Odin saw that he looked beaten and worn, as did the others. Fandral was badly wounded in the shoulder. He staggered, barely able to keep his feet. Volstagg, too, was wounded, with a blackened, frostbitten arm. Odin also saw that Laufey had begun to form a blade of ice in his right hand. The Jotun king was not willing to forgive Thor's offense. With two of Thor's companions wounded and the Asgardians outnumbered, Odin knew any full-scale battle might well end badly.

He knew what must be done. Laufey made his move, raising the ice blade and striking it toward Odin—but the All-Father was prepared. He raised his mighty spear, Gungnir, high over his head and slammed it down into the ice. The massive impact knocked back the advancing Frost Giants and caused the ice to break and crack. Odin then quickly called upon the Bifrost. Another hole ripped the sky, and before Laufey or the other Frost Giants could react, Odin pulled himself and the other Asgardians up and out of Jotunheim.

They were safe for the moment. But Laufey would not forget the insult Thor had dealt him. There would be war with the Jotuns.

And now Odin would have to deal with Thor.

As soon as they arrived back in the Observatory, Odin sent Lady Sif and the Warriors Three back to the palace. Fandral and Volstagg needed healing, and what Odin had to say was to be said only to family. Turning to his elder son, he looked for any sign that Thor was sorry for what he had done. A sign that he knew his actions were those of a bold and arrogant young man not yet ready to rule. But Odin saw none, even when he told Thor he'd been wrong for going to Jotunheim, and that he had almost put an end to a peace that had lasted for years. Even then, Thor just stood there, defiant as always.

"The Jotuns must know that the new king of Asgard will not be held in contempt," Thor said.

"That's pride and vanity talking," Odin said. "Have you forgotten everything I taught you? What of a warrior's patience?"

"While you're patient, the Nine Realms laugh at us!" Thor shouted. "You'd give speeches while Asgard falls!"

Thor's anger stoked Odin's temper. "You're a vain,

greedy, cruel boy," he growled, the words hot on his tongue.

"And you are an old man and a fool!" Thor shouted back.

Odin felt a great weariness wash over him. The trip through the Bifrost had taken more energy than he had left to give, and his son's words stabbed at him. "Yes," he said, his voice bitter. "I was a fool to think you were ready."

Odin did not act without thought. And he had thought through the past day's events quite thoroughly. He knew what he had to do, even if it meant losing his son forever. Thor needed to learn to be a true king. He needed to learn compassion and humility and patience, and he couldn't do that here in Asgard.

Thor needed to be stripped of his godly powers and sent to a realm where he would bleed and hurt like a mortal. He had to learn to put the needs of others before his own, so that he would be able to do the same for his people. There was no other choice. Thor needed to be sent to Midgard, the mortal realm whose people called it by another name: Earth.

Stepping forward, Odin went to stand in front of the panel that controlled the Bifrost. He plunged his spear into the device, and the Observatory began to hum with energy. Turning, he walked over toward his elder son as his younger looked on.

"You are unworthy of this realm," he said, ripping a disk off Thor's chest armor.

"Unworthy of your title…" He ripped away Thor's cloak.

"Unworthy of the loved ones you've betrayed." Odin's voice cracked with emotion as he went on. "I hereby take from you your powers." He held out a hand and Mjolnir flew into it.

Thor's eyes grew wide as the reality of the situation began to hit him. But his father wasn't finished. "In the name of my father," Odin continued, "and of his father before…

"I cast you out!" Odin exclaimed. The Bifrost glowed

strong, and in one swift move Odin pushed Thor through the portal. In moments, his son was gone from view.

Then, looking down at the hammer he still held, Odin quietly added, "Whosoever holds this hammer, if he be worthy, shall possess the power of Thor." With the last of his strength, he flung the hammer into the portal and watched it disappear.

A violent shaking then overtook Odin. Time was running out, and there was much at stake. Would Asgard once again be at war with Jotunheim? Would Thor ever learn his lesson and find his way back home? Would father and son ever reconcile?

And, most pressing, with Thor gone and Odin sleeping, who would rule the realm?

Odin did not act without thought. But as the Odin-sleep consumed him, he feared his thoughtful actions this time might mean the very end of Asgard....

A STRANGER'S
ARRIVAL

The air was dry and still. In Puente Antiguo, New Mexico, the stores were closed for the night, and the houses were quiet. The local residents were tucked inside, eating dinner and watching television. Parked on Main Street, which ran north and south through the center of town, was an old, beat-up utility vehicle. Darcy Lewis, a college intern working on Jane Foster's newest research project, sat in the driver's seat, swiping through social media posts on her phone. Jane's mentor and friend, Dr. Erik Selvig, read through various papers on his laptop in the passenger seat.

In the back of the van, Jane sat in front of a row of computer monitors and a variety of other scientific equipment. Most everything in the vehicle—including itself—had seen better days. The monitors were held together by duct tape, and some of the equipment was generations behind the most recent models—though Jane had managed to sneak in some very high-tech machines. As an astrophysicist who studied the stars for signs of spatial anomalies, she didn't have a lot of people pounding down the door to give her funding for research or equipment.

But that would change soon enough. She was sure of it. Her work here was getting her closer and closer to actual findings. And if tonight's readings were any indication, something big was about to happen. Something very big.

"Let's go," Jane said. Darcy put her phone away and started the van.

They headed into the dark desert. For a while, there was only the sound of the wind through the open windows and the occasional beep from the computers. Finally, about twenty miles outside town, the van came to a stop. They had arrived at their destination.

Jane popped the roof panels off the van and put her magnetometer on the roof. It would give her a reading about where the astral event would happen. There was a *thunk* below her, and Selvig said, "Ouch!" Then he stuck his head up next to Jane.

"So what's this anomaly of yours supposed to look like?" he asked.

Jane climbed onto the roof and got settled.

"It's a little different each time," she said. "Once it looked like, I don't know, melted stars pooling in a corner of the sky. But last week it was a rolling rainbow ribbon—"

"Racing round Orion?" Selvig teased her. "I always said you should have been a poet."

He was a colleague and friend of Jane's father, and he knew that her potential was limitless. He just wished she had chosen a field of study that was more easily accepted by the rest of the scientific community. While he had always believed in her, he feared her ideas might be too far ahead of their time for the rest of the world. Selvig's thoughts were interrupted by the beeping from one of Jane's devices.

The beeping increased, and Jane checked the magnetometer again.

"Here we go..." she said, excitement in her voice as she stared up at the sky. Selvig joined her. "In three... two...one...now!"

Nothing happened.

"Wait for it," Jane said.

Still nothing.

Leaning out the front window, Darcy looked up at Jane. "Can I turn on the radio?" she asked. It was pretty boring out there in the dark.

Jane shot her a look. "No," she snapped.

Frustrated, Jane sank back into the van. Selvig's expression was sympathetic. He knew how much this night had meant to Jane. He watched as she opened a notebook full of calculations. She didn't go anywhere without that notebook. It held her life's work. Which, at the moment, seemed useless. If she couldn't prove to

Selvig—who believed in her—that she had actual data that added up to something, she would never be able to convince a stranger. This was her last chance.

"The last seventeen occurrences have been predictable to the second, Erik!" she cried. She ran a hand through her light brown hair, her usually beautiful features marred by tension. "I just don't understand."

Turning back to her monitors, she began to rerun the calculations, looking for an error in her numbers, something, anything, to explain why nothing had happened. Focused on the screens, she didn't notice the odd glowing clouds that had formed in the sky. They came out of nowhere, their edges tinted in faint rainbow colors.

Darcy, however, did notice. "Jane?" she said over her shoulder.

"What?" Jane shouted back. Now was not the time to ask about music or if Darcy could do her nails or whatever else might be on Darcy's mind. "There's got to be a variable I haven't considered," she said, talking to herself. Displays on her equipment started to flicker and show obviously incorrect readings. "Or an equipment problem." She tapped one of the monitors, on the off chance that the problem was a loose connection she could jar back into place.

But then the whole van started to shake. Darcy said, "I don't think there's anything wrong with your equipment." Her tone was serious, so Jane lifted her head and looked through the front window.

Her jaw dropped.

In front of her was something unlike anything she had ever seen before. It looked as if the constellations had been sucked down from the sky and had gathered in a huge cloud. The rainbow light had grown stronger, brightening the area of the desert below the hovering cloud.

"That's your subtle aurora?" Selvig asked. He looked amazed.

"No—yes! Drive!" she shouted to Darcy before turning around and grabbing a camera.

As they raced through the night, Jane popped up out of the roof again and began filming. Her mind raced with the possibilities of what this could mean. Funding would be no problem once people got ahold of this footage. It was unbelievable. Then she frowned. Was it too unbelievable?

"You're seeing it, too, right?" she asked Selvig. "I'm not crazy!"

Popping his head up through the roof, he said, "That's debatable!" over the sound of the gathering storm. Jane relaxed. If Selvig was joking with her, that meant he believed her. He got serious only when he was questioning something.

The winds grew stronger. At the center of the clouds, a dark mass began to swirl faster and faster, forming a tornado. The strange rainbow light grew even brighter. "We've got to get closer!" Jane shouted to Darcy just as a huge bolt of lightning cut through the clouds and struck the ground. The van rocked on its wheels, and Darcy struggled to keep the vehicle level.

"That's it!" she cried. "I'm done! I'm not dying for six college credits!" Yanking the wheel with both hands, she tried to turn the van. But Jane wasn't about to let that happen. Jumping forward, she reached toward the wheel and tried to grab it. The two struggled for control while the wind outside whipped and howled. The van's headlights bounced over the desert, illuminating the form of a large man!

The man stumbled out of the storm, his clothes tattered and his eyes dazed. Looking up, Jane had only a moment to see confusion in his striking blue eyes. Jerking the wheel, she tried to avoid him, but—BAM! The van sideswiped the man, sending him flying.

The vehicle came to a stop, and a shocked silence filled the space as Jane, Darcy, and Selvig stared first at each other and then at the crumpled body on the ground. Then, as if jolted by electricity, they all leaped out of the van, Jane in the lead. She raced over to the man's side and knelt down, hoping and praying that she would find him breathing.

But she hadn't expected or hoped to find the handsomest man she had ever seen. His features looked as though they had been sculpted out of marble by a master. His chest was wide and his shoulders chiseled. His long blond hair lay undisturbed despite the windy conditions, and Jane had the overwhelming urge to run her hands through it. *I hit a model,* Jane thought, as she stared at him. *This is going to get me in so much trouble.*

"I think that was legally your fault," Darcy said.

Jane didn't have time to argue about it. "Get the first-aid kit!" she snapped. Darcy ran back to the van.

Jane leaned over the man and said, "Come on, big guy, do me a favor and don't be dead, okay?"

At the sound of her voice, the man groaned, and his eyelids fluttered. Then eyes of the deepest azure locked on Jane, and, for a moment, she forgot to breathe.

"His eyes..." she said.

"Are dreamy," Darcy said. She'd come back with the first-aid kit, but she wasn't thinking about it now.

Shaking her head, Jane rocked back on her heels. She needed to get a grip. She was more levelheaded than this. Clearly, this evening's events had made her a bit more emotional than she usually was, and the stress of hitting this guy was making her feel sympathy for him, nothing more. She was a scientist. Not some foolish young girl falling for a stranger. *Yes,* she thought, *it's just the night making me think foolish things.*

"We still need to get him to a hospital," Selvig said.

Jane sighed. "After we finish our readings?" she suggested.

But the night sky was clearing, and the wind calmed to an ordinary desert breeze. If Jane hadn't been right in the middle of it, she would never have known the night had turned so stormy. And why, she wondered, did it seem connected with this man lying in front of her?

Looking back down at him, she narrowed her gaze. Where had he come from?

A few uneasy moments passed. Then the man lying on the ground in front of Jane sat up abruptly, startling her. Staggering to his feet, he gazed down at his clothes, then up at the sky, and then back at Jane, who still sat on the desert floor. Stumbling from the impact, the stranger looked at them with a mixture of disappointment and disgust.

"Are you okay?" Jane asked, realizing even as she spoke that it was a rather silly question since he was obviously fine, though a bit disoriented. The blond man didn't answer. Instead, he continued to scan the ground. "Hammer," he said finally.

Jane didn't know what to say to that. She was about to respond, when, out of the corner of her eye, she saw odd markings etched in the sand near where the man had landed. "We've got to move fast, before anything changes," she said, her earlier excitement returning. Jane grabbed handfuls of soil samples, hoping to run a battery of tests on the earth when they got back to the lab. Then she realized it would be good to write everything down, so she reached for her notebook.

In fact, Jane was so absorbed in her work that she didn't notice Selvig and Darcy giving her odd looks. Finally, Selvig spoke. "Jane," he said gently, "we need to get him to a hospital." He nodded in the direction of the large man, who was wandering around the area, looking lost and sad.

Jane shook her head and kneeled down to scoop up another soil sample. "Look at him," she said absently. "He's fine."

"Father! Heimdall!" the man screamed, raising his hands to the sky. "Open the bridge!"

So maybe he wasn't completely fine. But Jane wasn't

about to waste time taking a mental case to the hospital when there was so much to go over here. "You and Darcy take him to the hospital," she said. "I'll stay here."

As she spoke, the man approached Darcy. "You!" he said, his voice booming in the quiet desert. "What world is this? Alfheim? Nornheim?"

"Uh...New Mexico," Darcy said, raising an eyebrow. What was this guy on? He may have been the hottest thing she'd ever seen, but he was seriously loopy.

Suddenly, he whirled, his expression furious. Darcy took an involuntary step back and reached into her pocket for the weapon she always carried with her. Holding it up in front of her, she tried to keep her finger from shaking.

"You dare threaten Thor with so puny a—"

Thor, as he called himself, didn't get to finish. Darcy fired, and he fell to the ground, convulsing with the electrical jolts. A moment later, he was unconscious.

Looking at the man on the ground and then at Darcy, Jane sighed. It seemed she would be going to the hospital after all.

Puente Antiguo was not busy, even in the middle of the day. But in the dead of night, it was practically a ghost town. The county hospital was no different. A few townies roamed the emergency room, having been dropped off after spending a bit too much time at the local tavern. The skeleton crew of nurses and doctors barely gave them any notice. Apparently, this happened almost every night.

What did not happen every night was having a man like Thor brought into the place. With considerable effort, Jane, Selvig, and Darcy managed to get him from the van and onto a gurney. Leaving the others to keep an eye on him, Jane made her way to the admitting area. A young nurse sat behind the desk, filing her nails. Jane cleared her throat.

Looking up, the nurse smiled. Then, in a manner that could only be described as painstaking, she began the process of admitting Thor.

"Name?" she asked, her fingers poised over the keyboard.

"He said it was Thor," Jane answered.

The nurse typed out each letter with one finger. T-H-O-R. "And your relationship to him?"

"I've never met him before," Jane said.

"Until she hit him with the car," Darcy added helpfully.

Jane shot her a look. "Grazed him, actually. And she stunned him," she quickly added, trying to make that sound worse than hitting him with her car.

"I'm going to need a name and contact number," the nurse said, either too tired or not bright enough to care that Jane had just admitted to hitting a man with her car. As Jane spelled out her name, the nurse once again slowly typed each letter. Click-click-click. Jane felt her shoulders tensing, and she was just about to scream when Selvig walked over and handed his card to the nurse.

"You can reach us there," he said simply. Then he turned and walked out of the emergency room, Jane and Darcy following.

They had done what they could for "Thor." There

was nothing left to do. It was now in the hands of the hospital.

Then why, Jane thought as they walked away, *do I feel like I shouldn't leave him?*

Sighing, she shrugged off the thought. She had tons of data to go through and soil samples to test. She had her hands full enough without the addition of a strange, albeit handsome, man. It was time to go back to her office and get to work.

When Jane had arrived in Puente Antiguo, there had been little in the way of free office space for rent. So she had settled on what there had been—an abandoned car dealership that had been empty for years. The old sign that read SMITH MOTORS still rose from the roof, a reminder of better days when the town had been more prosperous. Early the next morning, Jane sat hunched over a workstation. The sun rose over the distant mountains through the large windows behind her, making them gleam and sparkle. Jane didn't notice. She was busy soldering a piece of equipment while a printer churned out images she had taken of the previous night's storm.

"Darcy, take those soil samples to Professor Meyers in geology," Jane said. She put the cover back on the monitor and turned it on. It lit up, displaying a graph of overlapping squiggly lines under the heading "Algorithm Analysis." Jane studied it, waiting for an insight to jump out at her, while she waited for the images to finish printing.

Selvig walked into the lab holding two cups of coffee. He placed one in front of Jane and then took a sip from his.

"We might want to perform a spectral analysis," he suggested softly.

Jane looked up, surprised. "We?" she repeated. She wanted to squeal with excitement, but kept her composure.

"I flew all the way out here," Selvig said with a casual shrug. "Might as well make myself useful."

"You know what would really be useful?" Jane suggested. "If you still had your friend at the observatory ... they might have picked up gravitational waves from this, um ... event."

"You don't think it was just a magnetic storm?" Selvig asked.

"These anomalies might signify something bigger," she said, indicating an image on the monitor. It showed the giant cloud they had seen the night before. As the image shifted, the cloud disappeared, and a blisterlike object appeared in its place. It bulged outward like a balloon, and it appeared to be covered in stars. Jane waited for Selvig to absorb what he was seeing and then she spoke again. "I think the lensing around the edges is characteristic of an Einstein-Rosen Bridge."

Darcy, who had been doodling in her notebook while she waited for each of the pictures to print, looked up, confused.

"A wormhole," Jane explained in layman's terms. "A tunnel, pretty much, between different points in space. Only anything that goes through it gets from one point to another instantaneously."

What she didn't say was that it appeared the wormhole, if it was one, had opened into a place unknown to any scientist or astrophysicist. The constellation of stars they saw was brand-new. It didn't exist in any sky you could see from Earth.

A moment later, Darcy's voice broke into Jane's thoughts. "Hey, check it out," she said.

Jane turned, about to chastise Darcy for interrupting her, but the words died on her lips. Darcy was holding up a picture of the funnel cloud of stars. And there, in the middle of it, as if being shot down from the heavens like a bolt of lightning, was the unmistakable image of a man. Thor.

All three were silent as they tried to process what this meant.

"I think I left something at the hospital," Jane said finally.

Racing toward the door, she hoped that Thor would still be there.

When they arrived, room 102 was empty. The bed was overturned, and the IV stand lay on the ground.

Clearly, Thor had decided to check himself out. Sighing, Jane went back to the parking lot.

"Typical," she said. "I just lost my best piece of evidence."

"So, now what?" Darcy said when she saw that Jane was alone.

"We find him," Jane answered.

"Did you see what he did in there?" Selvig protested. "Finding him might not be the best idea."

Jane didn't care. "Our data won't tell us what it was like inside the event. He can."

This Thor person, whoever he was, was the most important piece of information Jane had. There was no way she was going to just let him disappear. Of course it had nothing whatsoever to do with the fact that he was incredibly handsome and had made her heart race wildly. No, it had nothing to do with that. It was all about the science.

"So we're just going to spend the rest of the day looking for him?" Selvig asked. He sounded skeptical.

"As long as it takes," she said, and yanked open the car door.

Getting in the driver's seat, she put the car in reverse, stepped on the gas, and—BAM! She hit something—again. With a groan, she looked in the rearview mirror. Thor! Dressed in hospital scrubs, he lay on the ground in a position eerily similar to the one from the night before.

Leaping out of the car, she raced around to the back and knelt down. "I'm so sorry!" she cried. "I swear I'm not doing that on purpose."

Thor didn't say anything for a moment. He simply gazed up at the sun, which was now high in the sky, its rays warming the pavement. "Blue sky, one sun," he said softly. Then he groaned. "Oh no. This is Earth, isn't it?"

A TOUCH OF
BLUE

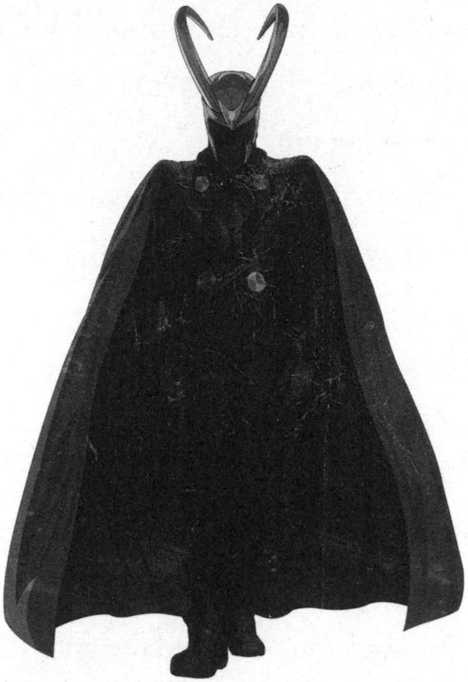

Loki could not stop looking at his arm. It looked normal now, but during the fight against the Jotuns there had been a moment when their icy blue coloration had spread across his flesh. Not as an infection, but as if the touch of one of Laufey's Jotun warriors had awakened something in Loki that only his body remembered. The blue color, and the chill that had come with it, were gone as soon as the Jotuns broke physical contact with Loki. He had told no one.

"We should never have let him go," Volstagg said. His normal boisterous spirits had given way to gloom.

"There was no stopping him," Sif said.

Fandral agreed. "At least he's only banished, not dead. Which is what we'd all be if that guard hadn't told Odin where we'd gone."

"How did the guard even know?" Volstagg asked.

There was a pause. Then Loki said, "I told him."

"What?" Fandral was shocked.

"I told him to go to Odin after we'd left," Loki said. "Though he should be flogged for taking so long."

Volstagg grew angry. "You told the guard?"

"I saved our lives!" Loki said. "And Thor's. I had no idea Father would banish him for what he did."

Sif, as always, was already looking for solutions. "Loki, you're the only one who can help Thor now," she said. "You must go to the All-Father and convince him to change his mind!"

"And if I do, then what?" Loki asked. "I love Thor more dearly than any of you, but you know what he is. He's arrogant. He's reckless. He's dangerous. You saw how he was today. Is that what Asgard needs from its king?"

None of them wanted to admit it, but Loki had a point. He waited for them to say something. When they didn't, he left the room. Sif and the Warriors Three watched him go.

"He may speak about the good of Asgard, but he's always been jealous of Thor," Sif said.

"True, but we should be grateful to him. He did save our lives," Volstagg pointed out.

Hogun, who spoke rarely, spoke then. "Laufey said there were traitors in the House of Odin."

"Why is it every time you choose to speak, it has to be something dark and ominous?" Fandral complained.

"A master of magic could easily bring three Jotuns into Asgard," Hogun said.

The other three looked at him, understanding what he meant. Loki could have done it. Who else in Asgard had more reason?

But it was unthinkable. "No, surely not," Volstagg said.

"Loki's always been one for mischief, but you're talking about something else entirely," Fandral added.

Sif tended to agree with Hogun. "Who else could elude Heimdall's gaze with tricks of light and shadow?"

Volstagg thought of something else. "The ceremony was interrupted just before Thor was named king." That was suspicious timing.

"We should go to the All-Father," Sif said.

"And tell him what?" Fandral wanted to know. That his son betrayed the throne? Oh, and by the way, he should go back on his banishment of Thor just because we want him to?"

"It's our duty," Sif insisted. "If any of our suspicions are right, then all of Asgard is in danger."

Down in the Vault, Loki thought he probably knew what Sif and the Warriors Three were talking about. They would suspect him by now. They had never trusted him. Few Asgardians believed Loki had the realm's best interests at heart—but they did not know him. He had only ever wanted to please Odin and prove himself worthy.

The Casket of Ancient Winters stood on its pedestal before the steel gate hiding the Destroyer. Loki walked to the pedestal and grasped it with both hands.

As he did, the blue color he had first seen in Jotunheim spread up his hands and arms. He felt it, a deep chill in his body, as though something inside him was being awakened by touching the Casket.

The gate hiding the Destroyer began to fold away into itself. The Destroyer stepped forth, its Odinforce flames beginning to glow. Loki ignored it. He felt the chill spreading with the blue color, all over his body. It covered his face, and he felt something change, even in his eyes.

"Stop!" came a commanding voice from the far end of the chamber.

Loki turned to see his father. Behind him he heard the Destroyer stop and step back behind the gate. It reformed in front of the gate, hiding itself away again.

There was pain in Odin's eyes, and regret.

"Am I cursed?" Loki asked. He needed answers. What was happening to him?

"No," Odin said. "Put the Casket down."

Loki did, replacing it on the pedestal. As he let it go, he felt warmth flood through his body again. He watched the blue color fade away from his skin.

"What am I?" he asked.

"You're my son," Odin answered.

"What more than that?" Loki demanded. He thought he knew the truth, but he wanted to hear Odin say it.

But Odin could not reply. Loki would have to do it for him. "The Casket wasn't the only thing you took from Jotunheim the last day of the war ... was it?"

Odin looked Loki in the eye. "No," he said. He sighed, knowing he would have to tell the whole story. Leaning on Gungnir for support, he began.

"In the aftermath of the battle, I went into the temple, and I found a baby. Small for a giant's offspring— abandoned, suffering, left to die. Laufey's son."

Loki was stunned by this revelation. He was not just

a Jotun, but the son of the Jotun king? The same king he had bargained with for his friends' lives?

"Laufey's son. . ." he repeated, as if by saying it aloud he could begin to make sense of it. "Why? The temple was littered with Jotun bodies. You were at war. Why would you take me?"

"You were an innocent child," Odin said—but Loki, so skilled in the arts of persuasion and lying, knew there was more to it.

"You took me for a purpose," he said. "What was it?"

Odin did not reply.

"Tell me!" Loki cried out, begging to know the truth. Everything he thought he had known about himself—and about the All-Father—was crumbling away.

"I thought we could unite our kingdoms one day, bring about an alliance, bring about a permanent peace...through you," Odin said. "But those plans no longer matter."

"So I am no more than another stolen relic," Loki said bitterly. "Locked up here until you might have use of me."

Odin shook his head. "Why do you twist my words?"

"You could have told me what I was from the beginning. Why didn't you?" Loki asked.

"You are my son. My blood. I wanted only to protect you from the truth."

Overtaken by anger and hurt, Loki said, "Why? Because I am the monster parents tell their children about at night?"

"Don't," Odin said.

"It all makes sense now. Why you favored Thor all these years," Loki said. He took a step toward Odin, growing more and more angry. "Because no matter how much you claim to love me, you could never have a Jotun sitting on the Throne of Asgard!"

Odin began to shake. Loki knew Odin was weak, but right now he did not care. He had been deceived. He had been a pawn of Odin's for his whole life. He wasn't even a real Asgardian.

Very well, Loki thought. *Now I know the truth. Soon enough, so will the rest of Asgard.* But first he had a few more plans to lay.

He walked past his father, toward the door that would lead up and out of the Vault.

"Listen to me!" Odin cried out behind him. "Loki!"

Loki heard a thump. He turned and saw Odin slumping against the wall. He slid down the wall and sprawled on the stairs leading up to the door. Strange trails of light swirled behind every motion, a sure sign that the Odinsleep was beginning.

Loki ran to him, all of his anger suddenly overcome by fear. He loved Odin. Even though Odin had lied to him, that love was still stronger than his hurt. He knelt next to Odin and gathered the sleeping All-Father in his arms.

"Guards!" he shouted.

A FEAST OF
DELIGHTS

Back at her trailer behind the lab, Jane rummaged through her drawers, hoping to find something that might come close to fitting Thor. She grabbed an old pair of jeans and a T-shirt and brought them into the lab and handed them to Thor. Nodding over her shoulder, she told him he could change in the back. Then she went to join Darcy.

A moment later, Thor walked back into the main

part of the lab, bare-chested and holding the shirt in one hand. Jane's mouth went dry.

"You know, for a crazy homeless guy, he's pretty cut," Darcy observed, glancing between Thor and Jane in amusement. She had worked for Jane only for a little while, but she had never seen her boss act like this. It made her seem less like a superscientist and more like a human being.

Walking over, Thor held up the shirt. A sticker on the front of it was peeling off. It read: HELLO, MY NAME IS DR. DONALD BLAKE.

Jane blushed and quickly ripped the sticker off. "My ex," she explained. "They're the only clothes I had that'll fit you."

Thor took the shirt back and put it on over his head. When he was fully dressed, he began to walk around the lab, glancing at the various schematics and drawings that covered the drawing boards and walls. He stopped in front of the collection of pictures from the storm Darcy had posted.

"What were you doing in that?" Jane asked, walking over and pointing to the picture in the center. Thor's outline could clearly be seen floating in the middle of the cloud.

Thor looked closer and then shrugged. "What does anyone do in the Bifrost?" he said dismissively.

Bifrost? Jane wrote the word in her notebook. Why did that sound familiar? And why did Thor act as though this was nothing special? Who was he? She felt a tug in her gut, as though the answer were staring her in the face. But she shrugged it off. She probably just needed some sleep.

Thor, on the other hand, needed food. "This mortal form has grown weak," he said.

A short while later, the four sat in a booth at the only diner in town. Thor hadn't been kidding. He really was hungry. There was enough food on the table in front of him to feed the whole group. There was a platter of steak and eggs, a tall stack of pancakes, and a dozen biscuits covered with gravy. Thor scooped up a mouthful of eggs and downed it with a large swig of coffee. "This drink," he said, "I like it." Then he threw the mug down to the floor, shattering it and causing the other patrons to jump in their seats. "Another!"

Jane looked over at the diner's owner and smiled apologetically. "Sorry, Izzy," she said. Then, turning back to Thor, she hissed, "What was that?"

"It was delicious," Thor said. "I want another."

He sounded like a petulant little boy. "Then you should just say so," she instructed, embarrassed by Thor's thoughtless behavior.

"I just did," Thor replied, looking confused.

"I meant just ask for it," she said.

As Thor took another bite of his pancakes, two locals entered the diner and took a seat at the counter. Jane had seen them around. Jake and Pete. They were known in Puente Antiguo for spending a bit too much time having fun. However, at the moment, they seemed calm. Smiling at Isabella, they ordered cups of coffee.

"You missed all the excitement out at the crater," Jake said loud enough for Jane to hear.

Pete nodded excitedly. "They're saying some kind of satellite crashed."

At the mention of "satellite," Selvig perked up. "What did it look like?" he asked, getting up and walking over.

"Don't know nothing about the satellite," Jake answered, "but it was heavy! Nobody could lift it."

At that, Thor leaped to his feet, rattling the dishes and causing Jane to almost choke on her coffee. His eyes were wild as he rushed over and put his face right in Jake's. "Where?" he demanded.

Jake gulped visibly and tried to back away from the strange man in front of him. "Uh—uh—about fifty miles west of here," he said, his voice shaking.

Thor grinned. Jake and Pete looked like his expression scared them even more. "But, um, I wouldn't bother," Pete said. "Looked like the whole Army was coming in when we left!"

Turning, Thor walked out of the restaurant.

"Where are you going?" Jane asked, rushing after him. This guy was acting stranger and stranger. But she couldn't risk letting him leave again. He still hadn't helped her.

"To get what belongs to me," Thor said. Then he

stopped, as though it had just occurred to him that he had no idea where he was going. He looked at Jane. "If you take me there now, I'll tell you everything you wish to know."

Jane raised an eyebrow. "Everything?"

"All the answers you seek will be yours—once I reclaim Mjolnir."

"Mjolnir?" Jane repeated quietly. What was Mjolnir, and why did it sound like something Selvig would mutter when he was angry?

As if he could read her mind, Selvig pulled Jane aside. "Listen to what he's saying," Selvig insisted. "'Thor.' 'Bifrost.' 'Mjolnir.' These are the stories I grew up with as a child...in Scandinavia!"

Jane looked back and forth between the two men. True, Thor could maybe answer her questions, but Selvig had never let her down. Maybe he was right, maybe this was a fool's errand. Maybe this "Thor" was just a delusional stranger who thought he was some kind of Viking.

"I'm sorry," she finally said. "I can't take you."

"I understand," Thor said. "Then this is where we

say good-bye." Taking her hand, he raised it gently to his lips and, after bowing to the others, walked off.

Jane watched him go, and for the first time in a long time, she wondered if her heart was more powerful than her head.

"Now," Selvig said. "Let's get back to the lab. We have work to do."

LONG LIVE THE KING

Sif led the Warriors Three to the throne room, where they waited for the elite Einherjar Guards to open the door and conduct them in. Looking down in proper deference, they approached the elevated throne and knelt. "All-Father," Sif said. "We must speak with you."

They looked to the throne and froze in shock.

On the throne, wearing his ceremonial helmet with

its great curving horns, sat Loki. In his right hand he held Odin's mighty spear, Gungnir.

"What is this?" Volstagg demanded.

"My friends," Loki said. "You haven't heard? I am now ruler of Asgard."

"Where is Odin?" Fandral asked.

"Father has fallen into the Odinsleep," Loki said sadly. "My mother fears he may never awaken again."

Sif changed her tack. "We would speak with her," she said, glancing at the Warriors Three as if to tell them to let her handle the conversation.

But Loki shook his head. "She has refused to leave my father's bedside," he said. "You can bring your urgent matter to me, your king."

"We would ask you to end Thor's banishment," Sif said simply. She knew there was little chance of success, but she had to ask.

"My first command cannot be to undo the All-Father's last," Loki said. "We're on the brink of war with Jotunheim. Our people must have a sense of continuity in order to feel safe in these difficult times."

Nothing could have been worse news. If only they

could have spoken to Odin, to make him aware of their suspicions about Loki…but now that chance was gone.

As Thor's friends, the Warriors Three and Lady Sif would now be under suspicion themselves—especially if Loki believed they knew he had permitted the Jotuns to enter Asgard and try to steal back the Casket of Ancient Winters.

"All of us must stand together, for the good of Asgard," Loki said. He looked at them, not saying anything else, but they knew what he meant.

He was telling them that he was in charge and that he would not tolerate any opposition.

"Of course," Fandral said before the more hot-headed Volstagg or Sif could say something to anger Loki.

The group bowed their heads and left the throne room. None of them spoke until they were well away, for fear that Loki would hear what they said.

There was only one thing they could do now. It was dangerous and uncertain, and it might not work. But the only alternative was to surrender Asgard to its enemies.

FINDING
ANSWERS

Jane Foster's life had been turned upside down overnight. First, she had discovered a man in the middle of the desert. A man who, according to pictures she had taken herself, had fallen to Earth out of a rainbow-colored tornado. Then this same man had made cryptic remarks in answer to all her questions, only to kiss her hand and disappear into the desert in search of a fallen "satellite."

Yet none of that had prepared her to walk back into

her lab at Smith Motors and find it being raided by what appeared to be government agents. In the parking lot, men ripped equipment out of her utility vehicle, transferring it into large black vans. More agents came out of the lab, holding boxes and files in their arms.

Jane rushed forward and burst into the lab, her heart pounding and her fists clenched. "What is going on here?!" she demanded.

One of the men stepped toward her. He was slight, with thinning brown hair and a warm, friendly face. He held out a hand. "Ms. Foster," he said, "I'm Agent Coulson, with S.H.I.E.L.D. We're investigating a security threat."

S.H.I.E.L.D.? What the heck was S.H.I.E.L.D.? Was it some part of the FBI or CIA that they kept hidden, like in those crazy cop shows? Jane had the uncomfortable feeling that this had something to do with Thor's arrival. It was too big a coincidence.

"We need to appropriate your equipment," Coulson went on, "and all your atmospheric data."

"By appropriate, you mean steal?" Jane snapped. As if it weren't obvious that they were taking whatever they wanted, with permission or not. "We're on the verge of understanding something extraordinary." She held up her notebook as proof.

Coulson leaned down and picked up the box at his feet. Then, reaching out, he snatched the notebook out of Jane's hand and placed it on top of the pile. "Thank you for your cooperation," he said, and turned to leave the lab. A moment later, the rest of the agents left as well.

Silence fell over the room as Jane, Selvig, and Darcy took in the damage. There was nothing left but a few small pieces of paper stuck beneath thumbtacks and a couple of loose pages of printer paper lying on the floor.

"Years of research, gone," Jane said, defeated. "They took our backups! They took the backups to our backups."

Selvig reached out a hand to comfort her, but she shook it off. He couldn't help her. No one could. Then she looked out the window and a sliver of hope blossomed. Across the street, she saw Thor. He hadn't made it to the crater yet after all.

Smiling, she raced outside. She had an idea. Thor was going to help her get her research back.

A few minutes later, she and Thor were in the van. The sun was beginning to set, and storm clouds were forming in the evening sky. Jane concentrated on the rough terrain, but out of the corner of her eye, she snuck glances at Thor. He looked excited, almost as though he were going into battle. Jane, on the other hand, wasn't as confident.

"I've never done anything like this before," she said, breaking the silence.

"You're brave to do it," Thor replied, glancing over at her. For the first time since she'd hit him, he gave her a genuine smile.

"They just stole my entire life's work. I really don't have anything left to lose," Jane said.

"You're clever," Thor said. "Far more clever than anyone else in this realm." She shot him a confused look. "You think me strange?" he asked.

Jane caught the laugh that threatened to bubble out of her. Strange? That was putting it mildly. "Who are you?" she asked, trying to change the subject, or at least to start getting answers.

Thor nodded. "You'll see soon enough," he said, looking up ahead.

Jane followed his gaze, and her eyes grew wide. They had found the satellite. Parking the van, Jane and Thor made their way to the edge of the valley ridge and lay down on their stomachs. Pulling out a pair of binoculars, Jane looked down. The valley was illuminated with bright lights that reached high into the night and spanned outward. Guard towers were set up with armed men sitting inside, while other men and women rushed about on the ground. A glass-walled command trailer was at the center of the station, and Jane could just make out something beyond it. It looked small and dark and was partially buried in the ground. The satellite! There were massive tubes and wires that snaked around the grounds, leading in and out of what appeared to be temporary offices. On the side of one of the buildings, Jane saw the word S.H.I.E.L.D. written in bold white letters.

She turned and looked over at Thor. It seemed what she was looking for and what he was looking for were in the same place.

Getting to his feet, Thor shrugged off his jacket and handed it to Jane. "You're going to need this," he said.

"Why?" Jane asked. As if in response, thunder rolled across the desert sky. Jane could have sworn Thor had commanded the thunder to do that.

"Stay here," he said, ignoring her question. "Once I have Mjolnir, I will return what they stole from you." He looked her deep in the eyes. "Deal?"

"No!" Jane yelled, surprising both her and Thor. "Look what's down there! You can't just walk in, grab our stuff, and walk out!"

"No," Thor agreed, and Jane felt her shoulders relax. And then he added, "I'm going to fly out."

Turning, he walked away, leaving Jane lying there with her mouth open. As he slipped into the valley, the first drops of rain began to fall.

.

S.H.I.E.L.D

Thor might have made it unseen to the outer walls of the complex, but lightning flashed and revealed him to the sentries. He had just made it through the outer fence, tearing it up from the ground. He fought off the first guards and ran for the building, aiming for an open door with a ramp leading up to it. When he got inside, another soldier was just coming out. Thor knocked him down and took away his weapon. It was long and black and poorly balanced. He wasn't sure whether he was supposed to throw it or hit someone with it.

A light hit him, and he turned to see a vehicle bouncing in his direction. Rain fell harder, visible in the light shining from near the driver's seat.

He took the weapon away from the soldier and flung it at the vehicle, which was like Jane Foster's, but smaller. And with no roof. The weapon smashed into the light and the vehicle careened out of control as its driver ducked away from the fragments of glass. It crashed into the wall and part of the tunnel fell in on it. Other soldiers came to help their comrade.

Thor moved quickly away from them, toward the center of the huge pit, where the main structure was. Lightning crackled from the hole left in the roof. Thor knew Mjolnir was within.

He was almost there when a huge soldier stepped around the corner and punched him hard in the jaw. Thor went down but sprang right back to his feet and charged the soldier. They smashed together through the wall of the tunnel and back out into the rain.

When they hit the ground, the impact separated

them. Thor got to his feet. So did the soldier. He was as big around as Volstagg, but a full head taller than Thor.

"You're big," Thor said with a grin. "I've fought bigger."

He grappled with the huge mortal, wrestling and landing punches as best he could. This was a real battle, not like the others. This man could give Thor, at least in his mortal form, real fight.

But Thor did not lose battles—on Asgard or Jotunheim or Midgard—and he did not lose this one. He got the enormous mortal down and lunged back toward the hole in the wall, but the man seized his ankle. Thor pivoted in his grasp and landed one last powerful elbow to the man's midsection. The man gasped as the blow knocked the wind out of him, and Thor scrambled back into the structure.

He tore through the wall, which was made of some kind of tough fabric he could almost see through. It peeled away from the boards supporting the structure in great sheets, and he threw it aside.

There. Mjolnir!

It sat half-buried in the mud, with spotlights shining

down on it through the rain. Energy, bright and blue, crackled from it toward Thor and up into the sky. The rain fell harder, pounding the earth into mud around Mjolnir as Thor approached it, a broad smile spreading across his face. More of the black-clad soldiers might be gathering around him, but Thor knew it wouldn't matter when he had Mjolnir in his hands again.

He reached down, and felt the leather-wound handle of the ancient Uru war hammer. It felt right in his hand, as if it were made to be there. Thor smiled, and lifted...

Mjolnir did not budge.

Shocked, he pulled harder. Mjolnir was his! Given to him by his father!

But taken away, there in the Observatory when they had returned from Jotunheim. *No*, Thor thought. *No!* He strained with all his might, muscles standing out in his arms and shoulders...but his mortal form could not move the mighty hammer from the ground. Runes glowed on the side of its head.

Thor dropped to his knees. Mjolnir had refused him, and he was in the hands of his enemies.

The All-Father still deemed him unworthy.

He did not resist when the black-clad soldiers came to take him away.

Watching from outside the fence, Jane had a decision to make. She could not save Thor...not right then. Live to fight another day, she thought.

And ran for the van.

DARKEST
HOUR

A short while later, the van screeched into the parking lot at Smith Motors. Jane leaped out and raced inside. "I can't just leave him there!" she cried when she saw Selvig and Darcy. The two had been attempting to clean up the mess left by the S.H.I.E.L.D. agents. Darcy, however, had been distracted by a children's picture book that had somehow been left behind.

Flipping through it, she half listened as Jane filled Selvig in on what had happened out in the desert.

Suddenly, a word on one of the pages caught her eye. "Hey! Look!" she shouted. The word looked an awful lot like the one Thor kept repeating. And above the word was an image of a hammer.

Jane walked over and grabbed the book from Darcy. "Where did you find this?"

Selvig answered, "In the children's section. I wanted to show you how ridiculous Thor's story is."

"Aren't you the one who's always told me to chase down all possibilities?" Jane said. "If that's really an Einstein-Rosen Bridge out there, then there's something on the other side. Advanced beings could have come through it before." Like Thor and his hammer, she added silently.

For a moment, no one said anything. Jane had never dared challenge her mentor before, but there were just too many signs pointing to the fact that Thor, whoever he was, was not from Earth. And now he was trapped by agents intent on covering up his existence.

Finally, Selvig spoke. "I don't know what any of this means, Jane," he said. "But I'll help you because it's you."

Sevlig didn't want Thor staying in Puente Antiguo. It was too dangerous...for all of them. But he also knew that Jane needed information from Thor. And despite his reservations, he knew that Jane would eventually guilt him into helping her.

Selvig grimaced at Jane, who let out a breath that she hadn't realized she was holding.

"Thank you, Erik," she said.

He nodded and went to make a call. Now all she could do was wait and hope whatever plan Selvig came up with would work.

Thor sat in a chair while one of the soldiers spoke to him. A small man, calm, not threatening. He asked Thor questions about places he had never heard of. He accused Thor of crimes, and Thor did not bother to respond. None of it mattered. If Thor could not lift Mjolnir, he was unworthy of his father's gift. He did not care what happened to him.

After interrogating him for what seemed like all night, the small man left. Thor lowered his head.

"I thought he'd never leave," a familiar voice said.

Thor looked up, startled. Loki was there! "Loki? What are you doing here? What's happened? Is it Jotunheim—?" Thor knew he had acted rashly. He hoped he could atone for his mistake.

But what Loki said next made that impossible. "Father is dead."

Thor was speechless. Loki went on. "Your banishment, the threat of a war with the Jotuns...it was too much for him to bear."

It was my fault, Thor thought. I did that. I killed my father, the All-Father of Asgard, because I was too stupid to listen. There were tears in his eyes.

"You mustn't blame yourself," Loki said. "I know you loved him." He paused and then added, "The burden of the throne has fallen to me now."

Loki ruled Asgard. Thor understood this. It made sense. It also gave him a small glimmer of hope. "Can I come home?" he asked.

With sorrow plain on his face, Loki shook his head.

"The truce with Jotunheim is conditional upon your exile. Mother has forbidden your return."

Thor was cast out from Asgard.

Forever. He lowered his head. No wonder Mjolnir had refused him. He was unworthy even to be called Asgardian.

"This is goodbye, brother," Loki said. "I'm so sorry."

"No," Thor said. "I'm sorry. Loki...thank you for coming here to tell me."

"Nothing could have stopped me," Loki said.

He vanished then, as the small man from S.H.I.E.L.D. came back into the room. "You have a visitor," he said.

Behind him, the older man who was Jane Foster's friend burst into the room. "Donny, Donny, there you are!"

Who was Donny? Thor wondered. Then he remembered the name tag on the shirt from Jane's closet. "It's going to be all right, my friend," Selvig said. "I'm taking you home."

Thor let Dr. Selvig lead him from the building. Along the way they passed a clutter of instruments and machines on a table. Thor spotted Jane's notebook and picked it up as they walked by. He was not a thief; he was returning it to its rightful owner.

When Loki left his brother, he did not return to Asgard. Instead he visited another realm. The last time he had been here, he had fought at Thor's side against the overwhelming numbers of the Jotun enemy.

Now he walked alone across the icy landscapes of Jotunheim, knowing that in some way he could not quite understand or accept...he was coming home.

He found his way to the ruined temple, still shattered after the last war. Inside it was dark, save for the shafts of pale light falling through holes in the damaged ceiling. Jotuns appeared from the darkness, surrounding him, but he paid them no notice. He walked deeper into the temple.

Here was where Odin had found him. Here was where his life had been wrenched off course. He was a child of war, a refugee, denied his true heritage. Now Loki would begin to set that right.

Ahead of him appeared Laufey, red eyes burning in the darkness. Loki stepped to him and looked up to meet Laufey's gaze.

"Tell me why I shouldn't kill you," Laufey said.

"I've come alone and unarmed," Loki answered.

"To what end?"

"To make you another proposition," Loki said.

Laufey's chin lifted as he understood. "So you're the one who let us into Asgard," he said.

Loki permitted himself the slightest of smiles. "You're welcome."

But Laufey was in no mood for any humor. "My men are dead, and I have no Casket," he said. "You are a deceiver."

Loki had heard that before.

Laufey reached out and seized Loki around the throat. Loki did not resist. This, too, had been part of his plan.

"You have no idea what I am," he said, as he felt the

chill of his Jotun nature spread from Laufey's gripping fingers through the rest of his own body.

Laufey stared in shock at Loki's transformation. The other Jotuns gathered in the temple shifted and muttered uneasily. Now Loki grinned. Everything was going precisely according to his plan.

"Hello, Father," he said.

"Ah," Laufey said. "I thought Odin had killed you. That's what I would have done. He's as weak as you are."

"No longer weak. I now rule Asgard, until Odin awakens," Loki said. He waited for this to register with the assembled Jotuns. Then he added, "Perhaps you should not have abandoned me so carelessly."

Laufey paused to consider this. "Or perhaps it was the wisest choice I've ever made. I will hear you."

It was time to make the deal. Loki led with the part of his offer that would be most tempting to Laufey. "I will conceal you and a handful of your soldiers, lead you into his chambers, and let you slay him where he lies," he said. "I'll keep the throne, and you will have the Casket."

Laufey studied Loki's face. The Jotun king was wise, and crafty. He knew there was more to the offer than what Loki had said so far.

"Why would you do this?" he asked.

"When all is done, we will have a permanent peace between our two worlds," Loki proclaimed. "Then I will have accomplished what Odin and Thor never could."

Laufey was pleased. "This is a great day for Jotunheim. Asgard is finally ours."

And this was where Loki had to clarify things a little. He had no intention of giving up the throne of Asgard, when he had just begun to rule.

"No. Asgard is mine," he said. Anger tensed the muscles in Laufey's face, but Loki went on. "The rest of the Nine Realms will be yours, if you do as you're told."

It was quite bold to speak to the Jotun king in this way, especially in his own temple. Loki knew it, but he also knew the chance to kill Odin would be too much for Laufey to pass up.

After a long moment, Laufey gave the smallest of nods. "I accept," he said.

Loki turned to leave. His business in Jotunheim was concluded, but there was much to do yet in Asgard.

As Loki emerged from the Bifrost in the Observatory, he felt Heimdall's gaze boring into him. "What troubles you, Gatekeeper?" he asked.

"I turned my gaze upon you in Jotunheim, but could neither see nor hear you," Heimdall said. His eyes never left Loki's. "You were shrouded from me, like the Frost Giants who entered this realm."

Loki knew perfectly well that Heimdall was accusing him of hiding the Jotuns, but he had no desire for open conflict now. He preferred to work by stealth and manipulation. "Perhaps your senses have weakened after your many years of service," he said, putting on a sympathetic air.

Heimdall did not let the point go. "Or perhaps someone has found a way to hide that which he does not wish me to see," he said.

Perhaps a more direct approach would be required

here, Loki thought. "You have great power, Heimdall," he said. "Tell me, did Odin ever fear you?"

"No," Heimdall said.

"And why is that?"

"Because he is my king, and I am sworn to obey him."

"Exactly," Loki said. "Just as you're sworn to obey me now. Yes?"

For a long moment, Heimdall did not reply. Loki was unarmed and Heimdall's hands held the double hilt of his great sword. It was a bad time for a battle.

But Heimdall's sense of loyalty—to his role as Gate-keeper and to Asgard—got the better of his suspicion toward Loki.

"Yes," he said reluctantly.

"Good," Loki said. "Then you will open the Bifrost to no one until I have undone what my brother has started."

With that he left the Observatory, but he felt Heimdall's all-seeing gaze on his back. Loki had a strong feeling that this was not the last time he and the Watcher of the Bifrost would come into conflict.

UNEXPECTED ALLIES

Jane didn't know what Selvig was planning or whether he would be able to get Thor out of the mess he had created by crashing illegally into the S.H.I.E.L.D. post. What would he tell them? What if they arrested Erik, too, and kept him along with Thor? Every time the wind blew or a car passed by the lab, Jane jumped. Finally, Darcy sent her to the trailer to get some rest, insisting that she'd tell her when Selvig and Thor returned.

Just as Jane was falling into a fitful sleep, there was a loud rapping on the door. Jumping up, she threw it open to see Thor standing there, Selvig thrown over one shoulder. Jane's hand went to her heart, and she let out a loud gasp. "What happened?" she said. "Is he...?" She didn't dare say the word aloud. But then Selvig groaned and mumbled something about gods of thunder and realms, and she caught an unmistakable odor.

It seemed Selvig and Thor had gone out to celebrate Thor's escape from S.H.I.E.L.D. She should have known.

Gesturing behind her, Jane stepped aside so Thor could come in. There was something different about him. He seemed quieter, less sure of himself. She wondered what had happened after she'd left the base to make him act this way. Gently, Thor placed Selvig on the bed and then patted the old man's cheek. *Yes,* Jane thought, *something must have happened.*

Then she realized Thor was no longer looking at Selvig but glancing around the trailer at the empty pizza boxes, old newspapers, and cookie wrappers. "Can we go outside?" Jane suggested.

Thor nodded, and they walked out of the trailer and headed over to the lab. On the roof, Jane had set up some chairs and a telescope and there were a few blankets.

"I come up here sometimes when I can't sleep," she explained. "Or when I'm trying to reconcile particle data. Or when Darcy's driving me crazy." She paused as a smile crept over Thor's face. "I come up here a lot, now that I think about it."

Thor didn't say anything. Instead, he just looked up at the night sky, as if it could provide him with answers. Once again, Jane was struck with the clear sense that the Thor she had known this morning was different from this Thor. This Thor seemed more human despite the impressive muscles.

Finally, he spoke up, his deep and somber voice in the stillness of the night startling Jane. "You've been very kind," he said. "I've been far less grateful than you deserve."

"I also hit you with my car a couple of times, so it kind of evens out," Jane said, teasing him.

Thor grinned and nodded. Then he reached into the

pocket of his pants and pulled out Jane's notebook. He held it out to her. "It was all I could get back," he said apologetically. "Not as much as I promised. I'm sorry."

Jane took the notebook and opened it gently, as though scared it would disappear again. He had no idea how important this notebook was. It meant that she wouldn't have to start from scratch. That she could still prove her hypothesis. It was the greatest thing he could have gotten back. "Thank you," she said softly.

Then her face clouded over.

"What's wrong?" Thor asked, concerned.

"S.H.I.E.L.D.," she answered. "Whatever they are, they're never going to let this research see the light of day."

"You must finish what you've started."

"Why?" Jane asked, surprised at the urgency in his tone. And the confidence.

"Because you're right," he said simply. "It's taken so many generations for your people to get to this point. You're nearly there. You just need someone to show you how close you really are."

As he spoke, Thor moved closer. Jane's heart

hammered in her chest as he reached over and took her notebook from her hands. Opening it to the image of what he called the Bifrost, he smiled. He was going to show her just how close she really was.

He drew a picture of Yggdrasil, the World Tree, from which all things sprang. Its branches reached out to the Nine Realms. "Your ancestors called it magic," he said. "You call it science. I come from a place where they're one and the same. Your world—this world, Midgard—is one of the Nine Realms, linked together by the branches of the World Tree."

He looked at her. She was listening. Also she was very beautiful, Thor thought. He kept talking, telling the story, just to keep her looking at him and listening.

In the banquet hall, Volstagg did what he always did. He ate. He cleared platters of food, threw them aside, and went on to the next. Sif stood looking out the window, ill at ease, trying to think of a way to get Thor back to Asgard without Loki's interference. Hogun and Fandral watched Volstagg, awed as always by his endless appetite.

Finally, Fandral couldn't stand it anymore. "Our dearest friend banished, Loki on the throne, Asgard on the brink of war, yet you manage to consume four wild boars, six pheasants, a side of beef, and two casks of ale. Shame on you!" he shouted. "Don't you care?"

He swiped Volstagg's latest platter off the table. Furiously Volstagg drew his sword. "Do not mistake my appetite for apathy," he warned.

Sif understood. Volstagg loved to eat, but right now he was eating because it made him feel good in the midst of a bad situation.

"Stop it, both of you!" she said. "We all know what we have to do. We're just too afraid to do it!"

This shamed them all. It was true. They were hesitating because they were afraid. That kind of fear was not worthy of an Asgardian.

"We must go," Hogun said. "We must find Thor."

"It's treason, Hogun," Fandral protested.

"Not to mention it's suicide," Volstagg added.

"Thor would do the same for us," Sif said quietly.

The Warriors Three fell silent. It was true. They owed it to their friend, and they owed it to Asgard.

But before they could act, an Einherjar Guard entered the banquet hall. Lady Sif and the Warriors Three tensed. Was this the moment when Loki would move against them?

"Heimdall demands your presence," the guard said.

Volstagg looked gloomy again. He was thinking what they all were thinking: If Heimdall had heard them discussing treason, they might be in very deep trouble indeed.

"We're doomed," he said.

One did not refuse a summons from Heimdall. They found him standing at his station, before the Observatory's controls. He stared at them for a long moment, until all four of them were thoroughly unsettled and nervous.

At last Volstagg spoke, just so someone would say something. "Good Heimdall, let us explain—"

Heimdall cut him off immediately. "You would defy the commands of Loki, our king, break every oath you have taken as warriors, and commit treason to bring Thor back?"

The four of them looked at each other, then back to Heimdall. What could they say? Volstagg nodded at Sif, trying to prompt her to say something. She was the one who usually spoke without putting her foot in her mouth.

She glared back at him, then looked to Heimdall. "Yes," she said, "but—"

Now it was her turn to be interrupted by Heimdall. "Good," he said.

For a moment they were sure they must have misunderstood him. But he said nothing else.

Eventually, Volstagg asked the question all of them wanted to ask. "So you'll help us?"

"I am bound by honor to our king. I cannot open the Bifrost to you," Heimdall said.

This was a letdown. Sif and the Warriors Three were once again confused.

Then Heimdall strode past them, leaving them alone in the Observatory.

"Complicated fellow, isn't he?" Fandral observed after a while.

Volstagg waited another moment. He still feared being overheard. Then he asked, "Now what do we do?"

Sif had been looking around the Observatory, frustrated at being so close to the Bifrost, yet still unable to help Thor.

Then she saw something. "Look!"

The others turned and saw what she was pointing at. They all started to grin at each other.

Heimdall had left the Observatory, but he had also left his sword in the controls. The message was clear: He was letting them use the Bifrost, at great danger to himself.

Now all they had to do was open it up and go find Thor.

Heimdall took up his station outside the Observatory, after Sif and the Warriors Three were gone. He had his sword again and feared he would have to use it...for Loki was approaching him on the short spur of the Rainbow Bridge that connected the Observatory to Asgard proper.

"Tell me, Loki," Heimdall said as Loki stopped a few feet in front of him. He carried Odin's spear, Gungnir. "How did you get the Jotuns into Asgard?"

Loki did not bother to deny the accusation. "You think the Bifrost is the only way in and out of the realm?" he said with a smirk. "There are secret paths among worlds to which even you with all your gifts are blind. But I have need of them no longer, now that I am king."

Then he grew more serious. "And, I say, for your act of treason, you are relieved of your duties as gatekeeper. And you are no longer a citizen of Asgard."

"Then I need no longer obey you," Heimdall said, and raised his sword. He had known this moment would come.

He struck at Loki, but Loki moved just a bit faster. Pointing Gungnir at Heimdall, he unleashed a storm of frost. Ice collected on Heimdall's armor, slowing the stroke of his sword. Heimdall pushed forward with all his strength, baring his teeth with effort. Still his great sword moved, but more and more slowly. Loki's skin turned blue and his eyes took on the red color of his true father, Laufey.

Heimdall was a fearsome warrior, but even he was not quite strong enough to overcome the combined power of Gungnir and Loki's magic. He was frozen solid, with the edge of his sword scant inches from the side of Loki's throat.

Loki paused. Gradually, the Jotun blue left his skin and his eyes returned to their normal green color. That had been closer than he would have wanted. He leaned away from Heimdall's sword and turned on his heel.

There was one final task to complete.

The Vault was silent. The Cask of Ancient Winters stood on its pedestal. Loki stepped around the pedestal and gestured toward the gate holding the Destroyer back.

The gate folded away into itself and the Destroyer stepped forward.

"Ensure my brother does not return," Loki said.

A NEW TALE
TO TELL

The next morning, Jane woke and stretched. Then she opened her eyes and smiled. Thor slept next to her, the rising sun turning his blond hair golden. They had stayed outside all night talking about the Rainbow Bridge, the Bifrost, and the Nine Realms of Yggdrasil, including Asgard, where Thor was from, and Midgard, or Earth. Her mind was spinning with information, yet she also felt oddly at peace. Thor had opened Jane's eyes to so many things, and she had opened her life up to him. She wondered what that would mean for their future.

Beside her, Thor let out a small sigh and then his eyes fluttered open. Looking over at her, he smiled. "Breakfast?" he suggested.

A half hour later, the smell of bacon and pancakes filled the lab. Jane sat at a table with Selvig and Darcy, trying to explain everything Thor had taught her. At the kitchen sink, Thor happily attempted to do the dishes. Jane looked over at him, impressed.

"They're fascinating theories, Jane," Selvig said, looking at the new notes in her book. "But you're not going to be able to convince the scientific community of any of this, if you don't have hard evidence to back it up."

Jane was about to reply when a S.H.I.E.L.D. agent entered.

There was a knock on the door before the agent stepped out of the doorway and they all found themselves looking at three brawny and dangerous-looking men, plus a woman who was even more dangerous looking than any of the men.

"My friends!" Thor cried, a delighted smile breaking across his face. Breakfast forgotten, he rushed over to let the group in.

The first to enter was the widest of the group. He had a long beard and a big belly, and he wore odd armor that looked ancient and futuristic at the same time. From their talk the night before, Jane assumed these were Asgardian warriors come to rescue Thor. The big man's next words confirmed her thoughts.

"Lady Sif and the Warriors Three," he said, his voice jolly. "Surely you've heard tales of Hogun the Grim, Fandral the Dashing, and I, Volstagg the Svelte?"

Jane stifled a laugh while Selvig raised an eyebrow and gave Volstagg's belly a look.

"Perhaps I've put on a little more muscle since I was here last," he said, sounding a bit hurt.

"That would have been a thousand years ago? Northern Europe?" Jane said, looking over at Darcy and Selvig as if to say, "I told you so."

Volstagg looked thrilled to be remembered. "Exactly!" he said, smiling.

Thor had been oddly quiet since Lady Sif and the Warriors Three had arrived. Now he walked over and put an arm around Volstagg. "My friends," he said, "I've never been happier to see anyone. But you should not have come."

The warrior called Fandral looked confused. "We're here to take you home," he said.

"You know I can't go home," Thor said. "My father is dead because of me. I must remain in exile."

Sif and the Warriors Three looked at one another, puzzled. "Thor," Sif said. "Your father still lives."

Jane saw the pain flash across Thor's face. He had not told her everything about the events that had brought him to Earth. But he had said that his actions had caused his father, Odin, to banish him and to strip him of his godly powers, making him mortal. Her heart ached for him. She almost stepped forward to reassure him, but she stopped.

Lightning flashed across the sky, and the distant

sound of thunder boomed. But it was not a storm—it was the Bifrost. Something had followed Lady Sif and the Warriors Three to Midgard. Something much more terrifying.

The sky grew even darker and the wind howled, sending trash dancing along the streets and causing people to duck into buildings for shelter. Jane felt the hairs on the back of her neck stand up. She was frightened, but she was determined not to show it, especially not in the face of Asgardian warriors.

"What is it?" she asked.

Thor looked grim. "I don't know," he said sadly. "Perhaps this is another one of Father's lessons that I just don't understand." His eyes suddenly flashed, showing his determination to do the right thing. "Jane, you must leave now."

She shook her head. "What are you going to do?" she asked.

Before he could reply, Volstagg stepped forward. "He's going to fight with us, of course!"

Thor's shoulders sank and he turned back to his friends. "Not today," he said softly. "I'm just a man."

Then, as though comfortable with his fate, he added, "You must stop this on your own. I'll stay and help evacuate this town. But we'll need some time."

"You'll have it!" Volstagg cried.

With a salute to the humans—and Thor—they walked out of the lab and into the growing storm.

As soon as they had left, Thor and the others jumped into action. Racing out into the street, Jane began loading people into various vehicles with directions to get as far out of town as possible. At first, some of the townsfolk balked, but when they saw the storm in the distance, they nodded and got in the cars. Meanwhile, Selvig cleared out Isabella's diner and Darcy rushed to the bus station to tell the drivers where to go.

Soon, the place was virtually empty, more like a ghost town than ever before. Satisfied they'd gotten everyone out, Jane, Thor, and the others gathered in the back of the lab. They could hear the sounds of battle, and Jane saw Thor flinch as one of his friends let out a shout.

Thor could stand it no longer. He stormed out of

the lab and onto Main Street. Jane, Darcy, and Selvig followed.

What they saw astonished them. Puente Antiguo's downtown was already in ruins. Fires burned and cars were overturned.

And in the middle of it all stood the Destroyer.

How had Loki gained control of it? It should only have been responding to threats against Asgard! It must have truly believed him king of Asgard, with the All-Father gone into the Odinsleep.

It was nearly impossible to defeat the Destroyer, even for Asgard's mightiest warriors. In his mortal form, Thor couldn't imagine what he could do to help. But he was determined to find a way.

After Loki had sent the Destroyer over the Bifrost to Midgard, he waited in the Observatory. Heimdall, still frozen at his post, was poor company. "What's it like, Heimdall, to know what is happening and not be able to do anything about it?" Loki asked.

Only Heimdall's eyes moved. ·

"Such a pity," Loki said. He shifted the Observatory controls and opened the Bifrost again.

Laufey and two other Jotuns emerged.

"Greetings, Father," Loki said.

From a block down Main Street, Thor watched as Fandral executed a battle move Volstagg called the Flying Mountain. It was more or less exactly what it sounded like. Volstagg ran toward Fandral, who knelt and made a stirrup of his two hands. Volstagg stepped into it, and Fandral heaved him in the direction of the Destroyer. It was a devastating, unstoppable move, even if it tended to be hard on Fandral's back. No enemy could stand against the hurtling mass of Volstagg.

Except the Destroyer, which swatted him away as if he were an insect. He tumbled through the air and smashed down onto the hood of a parked car. The Destroyer's flame began to glow. In another moment it would incinerate Volstagg where he lay stunned by the blow.

At the very last second, Lady Sif leaped from the roof of the nearest building, spear held in both hands. She put all of her strength into the thrust, driving the point of the spear through the back of the Destroyer's neck and straight down into the street. The Destroyer slumped and went inert, as Sif landed on its back and steadied herself.

Volstagg grinned at her. It was not the first time she'd saved his life. All of them were always there for one another.

They relaxed for a moment…and then the Destroyer started to move again.

Its head began to turn, all the way around like an owl's. The bands of its armor spun and reoriented themselves so that within seconds it was bent backward over Sif's spear instead of forward. The furnace within its helmet glowed, and the roar of its gathering fire spurred Sif to leap aside just as it shot a bolt of fire through the space where she had been.

The Destroyer pulled itself up slowly until it was loose from the spear that had impaled it. It turned again and raked the street with its fire. Cars flew everywhere, and so did Sif and the Warriors Three as they were blasted by the irresistible Odinforce flames.

Thor had to act. "Go now. Run!" he said to Jane.

She did, with Darcy and Selvig. Thor ran, too, in the other direction—toward where Sif had fallen.

"Lady Sif," he said as she struggled to get up. "You've done all you can."

"No," she said through gritted teeth. "I will die a warrior's death. Stories will be told of this day."

Thor stopped her from charging off toward the Destroyer. "Live, and tell those stories yourself," he said. "Now go. You must return to Asgard. We have to stop Loki."

"What about you?" Sif asked.

"Don't worry, my friends." Thor looked back toward the Destroyer. It was searching for them at the other end of Main Street. "I have a plan."

As his friends, both Asgardian and mortal, fell back toward the abandoned Smith Motors building, Thor walked down the middle of Main Street. The Destroyer approached from the other direction, looming through the smoking wreckage and kicking aside cars.

Jane called to the others to wait. "What's he doing?"

"Brother," Thor said. He spoke to the Destroyer, but he knew Loki could hear him. "Whatever I have done to wrong you, whatever I have done to lead you to do this, I am truly sorry. But these people are innocent. Taking their lives will gain you nothing."

He stopped, looking up at the Destroyer, which had also stopped. They were less than ten feet apart. The front of the Destroyer's helmet opened up, and the fires within roared to life.

Undaunted, Thor went on. He had learned something in his time on Earth. True valor was not in simple fighting. It lay in knowing when not to fight, and knowing when to lay your life on the line for your friends.

"So take mine and end this," Thor said.

A long moment passed. Thor steeled himself for the consuming blast of fire that he was sure would come.

But then the Destroyer powered down. It turned around and took a step back toward the place in the desert where the Bifrost had brought it to Earth.

Thor took a breath. Whatever had come between him and Loki, they were still brothers.

That was what he was thinking when the Destroyer stopped, turned around, and backhanded Thor with all its strength. Thor flew through the air and crashed back onto Main Street more than a block away, unmoving.

"No!" Jane shouted. She ran to him, with the rest of Thor's friends close behind. The Destroyer strode away, out of Puente Antiguo and back into the desert.

Jane knelt next to Thor. His eyes fluttered open. He was badly hurt.

"It's over," he said. Speaking was hard for him, she could tell. Was he dying? He couldn't be.

"It's not over," she said.

"I mean you're safe," Thor said. He was fading.

"No," Jane said, weeping. Tears stood on the faces of Sif and the Warriors Three as well. They could never have imagined Thor struck down in battle.

Then they all heard something. It was like the sound of a falling rocket.

Or the sound of thunder.

They looked up into the sky and saw something falling toward Thor, almost faster than their eyes could track it.

"Jane!" Selvig cried out. He tried to pull her away from Thor, but she wouldn't leave.

At the last moment before the falling object struck … Thor's hand reached up to catch it!

Lightning flared around him, touching but not hurting any of the mortals or the Asgardians. It crackled around Thor, and they saw him change. His clothing disappeared and a shining suit of armor replaced it. A rich red cloak appeared draped over his shoulders as he sat up, and a winged helmet covered his head. In his right hand he held Mjolnir.

All of them thought they could almost hear words, like a voice was speaking distantly in all of their heads. *Whosoever holds this hammer, if he be worthy, shall possess the power of Thor.…*

Thor stood and looked around, his wounds healed

and his true Asgardian nature revealed on Earth for the first time. By sacrificing himself for his friends, he had proved himself worthy again.

"Oh...my...God," Jane breathed.

Thor smiled at her, but on the edge of Puente Antiguo, the Destroyer sensed that Thor was not yet dead. It turned and rushed toward him.

With a battle cry, Thor flung Mjolnir at the Destroyer, knocking it off-balance. It recovered, and blasts of fire struck all around Thor as Mjolnir returned to his hand. Whirling it over his head, Thor rose into the air. A storm gathered around him, growing more intense as Mjolnir created a whirlwind. The Destroyer was lifted off the ground. Again and again it blasted at Thor, and every time he blocked its fire with Mjolnir.

As the Destroyer rose higher, Thor dove down through the whirlwind to meet it, holding Mjolnir before him and forcing the Destroyer's fire back into it. Mjolnir blocked the opening in its helmet. The fire built inside the Destroyer until a huge explosion blinded everyone on the ground. They flinched away.

When they could see again, the Destroyer was

falling back to Earth. It landed with a huge crash and lay still.

Thor landed a few seconds later, the thrill of the battle still clear on his face. Jane had liked his looks before, but now he was a sight to behold. "Is this how you always look?" she asked.

Thor shrugged. "More or less."

She admired him a little more. "It's a good look."

They shared a brief moment before Thor returned his attention to what needed to be done. "We must go to the Bifrost site," he said. The Warriors Three and Sif prepared to go with him.

Before they could leave, a big black car pulled up and several S.H.I.E.L.D. agents got out, including the small man who had questioned Thor the night before. "Excuse me!" he said.

Thor turned to see what he had to say. As the man approached, he took in Thor's new appearance, and said, "Donald, I don't think you've been completely honest with me."

Thor had heard the small man's name in the buildings surrounding where Mjolnir had fallen to Earth:

Coulson. "Know this, son of Coul," Thor said. "You and I, we fight for the same cause: the protection of this world. From this day forward, count me as your ally...if you return the items you have stolen from Jane Foster."

"Not stolen," Coulson said. "Borrowed. You'll get your equipment back," he said to Jane. "You're going to need it to continue your research."

"I, um...what?" she asked.

"It's going to be very important," Coulson said to her, but he was still watching Thor and the other Agardians.

Thor could wait no longer. It was time to return to Asgard. "Would you like to see this bridge we spoke of?"

"Uh...sure," she said.

A few minutes later they stood at the great circle inscribed on the desert. This was the place where the Bifrost would open. Thor looked up into the sky and called out, "Heimdall, open the Bifrost."

Nothing happened. "He doesn't answer," Fandral observed.

"Then we are stranded," Hogun said.

Thor wasn't ready to give up. "Heimdall, we need you now!"

In the Observatory, Heimdall struggled with all his might against his icy prison. He could hear Thor's voice, but Loki's magic held him fast. Asgard needed him. Would his strength fail him now, at this crucial moment?

No! He shattered the bonds of ice and struck down the Jotun guard waiting for Laufey's return. The cold began to leave his limbs, and he felt his strength returning. There would be a battle coming…but first he had to answer the call of Thor.

Outside Puente Antiguo, the sky crackled open in a storm of color and energy. Selvig and Jane gasped. At last they were seeing the mythical Bifrost!

"I must go back to Asgard," Thor said to Jane. "But I give you my word, I will return for you. Deal?"

She answered him with a kiss. Thor's heart thrilled to it. He had never imagined having feelings for a mortal woman. The Nine Realms held many mysteries.

"Deal," Jane said when they broke away from each other.

And then it was time to go.

BROKEN

In the chamber where the All-Father lay deep in the Odinsleep, Frigga sat by her husband's bedside. She had seen him succumb to the Odinsleep before, but this was deeper and more sudden than usual. She was deeply concerned and afraid for him. With Thor gone, and Odin sleeping, Asgard was vulnerable to its enemies.

From outside the chamber, she heard the shout of the guards and the clash of weapons.

The doors burst open and a Jotun charged in. Frigga took up a sword leaning nearby and struck at it. The blade bit deeply into its shoulder but it batted her aside. She hit the wall and lay stunned.

Behind it, another, much larger Jotun came in... and behind it came Laufey.

The Jotun king approached Odin and lifted the lid of Odin's one eye. The eye did not respond; Odin was too far into the Odinsleep to respond.

"It's said you can still hear and see what transpires around you. I hope it's true, so you may know your death came at the hand of Laufey," he said. In one of his hands he had formed a blade of ice. He raised it slowly, relishing the moment.

A blast of energy hit Laufey from behind, shattering the ice blade and knocking the Jotun king to the floor. He looked up to see his attacker.

It was Loki! He stood with Odin's spear, Gungnir, leveled at the wounded Jotun. Around Gungnir's tip crackled fierce energy.

"And your death came by the son of Odin," Loki said, and unleashed another blast. Laufey lay still.

The huge Jotun that accompanied Laufey lunged at Loki then and would have done him in—but it stopped short, its mouth opening in surprise. It toppled over slowly, revealing Frigga, holding the sword she had used to cut it down.

Loki rushed to her, seeing she was hurt. "I swear to you, Mother. They will pay for what they've done today."

"Mother!" cried a familiar voice at the door.

Loki turned to see Thor in the doorway, looking at the scene with amazement.

"Thor!" Frigga said. She ran to him and embraced him. "I knew you'd return to us."

Loki saw that Thor held Mjolnir. He did not know how it had happened, but he knew it was not good for him.

"Found its way back to you, did it?" he said to Thor, nodding at the hammer.

"No thanks to you," Thor said. Frigga looked from one of her sons to the other. "Why don't you tell them how you sent the Destroyer to kill my friends?" he asked Loki. "And to kill me."

"It must have been enforcing Father's last command," Loki said, but he could see neither his mother nor his brother believed him.

"You're a talented liar, brother," Thor said. "Always have been."

Loki smiled at this. It wasn't the compliment he would have wanted, but it was true.

"It's good to have you back," he said. "Now, if you'll excuse me."

He raised Gungnir and unleashed a bolt of energy that blew Thor through the wall and out into the court-yard far below. Frigga screamed, but Loki was already on his way out of Odin's chamber.

Loki had killed Laufey. Now the only thing to do was take care of the rest of the Jotuns. He had to end the coming war before it started.

Thor got to his feet and saw Loki racing across the Bifrost spur toward the Observatory. A moment later, the Observatory shifted and aimed. Its energy was unleashed, and a beam of rainbow power arrowed out into space...pointed toward Jotunheim.

Thor swung Mjolnir upward and catapulted himself up onto the Bifrost spur.

The Observatory's controls were encased in a huge version of Yggdrasil, the World Tree. It was made entirely of ice, and its thicket of roots held the controls in place. Thor would not be able to break it without destroying the controls, too.

"You can't stop it," Loki said proudly. "The Bifrost will build until it rips Jotunheim apart."

"Why have you done this?" Thor shouted over the sound of the Bifrost's increasing energy.

"To prove to Father that I am the worthy son!" Loki answered. "When he wakes, I will have saved his life. I will be proved a worthy heir!"

"You can't kill an entire race!" Thor could not believe Loki would do such a thing. The Bifrost would soon destroy Jotunheim, and with it every Frost Giant. It was unthinkable.

"What is this love for the Jotuns?" Loki asked. "You, who went seeking war."

"I've changed," Thor said simply. It was true. At the moment of his banishment from Asgard, he had still been foolish and stupid. He had learned much in his short time on Earth.

Loki scoffed. "So have I," he said, and struck Thor across the face with Gungnir. It was a soft blow, meant to provoke Thor.

"Fight me," Loki demanded.

But Thor contained his temper. "Is the throne worth what you've done?" he asked.

"I never wanted the throne. I wanted only to be your equal." Loki hit him again. "Now, fight me!"

Thor held himself back. "I will not fight you, brother."

"I am not your brother!"

Thor couldn't understand how Loki had become so consumed with jealousy. "Loki, this is madness," he said.

"Is it? What happened to you on Midgard that turned you so soft?" Loki's expression changed. "Ah. It was a woman." He grinned. "Perhaps when we're done here, I'll pay her a little visit myself."

Thor had tried to restrain himself, but the threat to Jane was more than he could handle. He readied Mjolnir, and this time when Loki attacked him, Thor fought back. They battled back and forth with hammer and spear under the gleaming branches of the ice tree.

Loki battered Thor with Gungnir, the enchanted tip of which could pierce even Thor's armor. Thor smashed him back with Mjolnir. Loki skidded across the Bifrost and slipped over the edge! He was barely hanging on.

"Brother, please!" he cried out in fear.

Thor reached to help his brother...but it was an illusion! Loki was actually behind him and hit him hard enough that Thor himself nearly fell off the bridge. Thor got his balance and spun around.

He was surrounded by twenty Lokis. All laughed and mocked him. Loki had created illusions of himself!

Enough, Thor thought. He raised Mjolnir and brought down a stroke of lightning. The blast knocked all the Lokis down. The illusions disappeared, leaving only the real Loki behind.

Before Loki could get up, Thor laid Mjolnir on his chest, pinning him in place. Because no one but Thor could lift Mjolnir, Loki could not move the hammer or get out from under it.

Then Thor went to the icy tree, fighting the surge of Bifrost energies and trying to get close enough to free the controls and turn the beam away from Jotunheim. There would not be much time. Soon Jotunheim would be destroyed.

"Look at you!" Loki said, mocking Thor even though he lay pinned by Mjolnir. "The mighty Thor, with all your strength, but what good does it do you now? There's nothing you can do!"

But Loki was wrong. There was one thing Thor could do.

He reached out his hand and called Mjolnir to him. The hammer's handle smacked solidly into Thor's palm, and he raised Mjolnir to the skies. Thunder rumbled over Asgard and lightning arced from Mjolnir's head.

Thor brought the hammer down on the Rainbow Bridge. The blow was like an earthquake, shaking everything from the Observatory all the way down to the Vault, far underground, below Asgard's throne room.

Loki scrambled to his feet. "If you destroy the Bridge you'll never see her again!" he screamed.

Thor ignored him. Loki picked up Gungnir and ran toward Thor as Thor raised Mjolnir again.

"Forgive me," he said, and brought the hammer down again.

The blow shattered the bridge into millions of glittering fragments. The blast wave rolled out from the break point, rolling over the Observatory and tearing pieces of it away. The great gyre powering the Bifrost spun slowly down. The beam of energy shooting out from it toward Jotunheim faded away.

The explosion hurled Thor and Loki backward, tumbling them both over the edge of the bridge. Thor caught the edge and held on, but Loki was too far away. Stretching as far as he could, Thor reached his other hand and grabbed onto Gungnir. He held the spear with Loki dangling from its other end over the infinite space that stretched among the Nine Realms.

Thor's grip began to slip. He fought to hang on—and then a strong hand grasped him around the forearm.

He looked up and was astonished to see—Odin!

Awakened from the Odinsleep and looking younger, stronger, more vital than ever.

The raging storm of energy pouring from the broken bridge still raged. "I could have done it, Father!" Loki cried over the roar. "For you! For all of us!"

"No, Loki," Odin said. He did not raise his voice, but somehow it carried over the chaos anyway. Sadness, regret, and a father's disappointment were clear on his weathered face.

Thor wondered what the All-Father was saying no to. But he was never to find out, because Loki saw their father's expression. Thor looked from Odin down to his brother just in time to see Loki realize what he had done. He had betrayed the father who had raised him; he had opened Asgard to its enemies; he had nearly destroyed another realm; he had nearly killed his brother.

The burden of it was too much for Loki. Thor saw Loki make a choice.

"No!" Thor shouted, but perhaps Loki did not hear him. Or perhaps it made no difference.

Loki let go and fell away into space, swallowed up in

the endless spaces among the Nine Realms and swept away by the surging energies pouring from the broken bridge.

Odin pulled Thor up onto the Bridge. Thor staggered and fell against his father. He dropped Gungnir, and then dropped Mjolnir.

"It is over," Odin said.

EPILOGUE

There was a great feast in Asgard two days later. War with the Jotuns had been averted! Odin had awakened from the Odinsleep more quickly than anyone could have expected! Thor had returned, his banishment lifted!

Only the treachery of Loki hung over the festivities... and, of course, Loki's death. For surely he was dead, wasn't he? Sif thought so.

She could see Frigga thought so as well. The queen

was looking out from a corner of the banquet hall, a quiet spot far from the main party. "My Queen," Sif said. "I'm so sorry for your loss."

Frigga nodded. Sif looked out the window, too, and saw that the queen was watching her husband and her surviving son. Odin and Thor stood together on the shattered Bifrost spur, looking out over Asgard. Beyond them she could see Heimdall, standing his eternal watch at the very edge of the broken bridge.

"How is he?" Frigga asked. Of course she was asking about Thor.

"He mourns for his brother…and he misses her. The mortal," Sif said.

Again Frigga nodded. They all had suffered losses because of Loki.

"You'll be a wise king," Odin said. He was planning to complete the ceremony soon. It was time to hand the throne of Asgard over to his son.

"There will never be a wiser king than you," Thor

said. "Or a better father. I have much to learn. I know that now. Someday, perhaps, I shall make you proud."

Odin turned to him and rested a hand on his shoulder. "You've already made me proud."

He left Thor then, and Thor walked to the broken edge of the Bifrost. Heimdall was there. For a moment Thor looked at the stars. "So Earth is lost to us," he said.

"No," Heimdall said. "There is always hope."

"Can you see her?" Thor asked. He could, in his mind. He hoped Jane Foster thought of him as much as he was thinking about her.

"Yes."

"How is she?"

Heimdall paused as if considering how to say something. "She searches for you," he answered.w

Thor couldn't help but smile at this. He would see her again. As Heimdall had said, there was always hope.

TURN THE PAGE FOR AN EXCITING PREVIEW OF

MARVEL CINEMATIC UNIVERSE
PHASE ONE

MARVEL

THE INCREDIBLE HULK

He remembered the green light of the scanner playing across his face. He remembered the feeling of the gamma radiation, like a tingling heat on his skin. He remembered being scared when he felt his body start to change.

After that, things were confused. There was a chair smashing through a window. Wrecked lab equipment scattered across the room. Betty slumped on the floor. Crushed lab furniture and computers jumbled on top of *the two people beside her. General Ross, his uniform torn, scrambling.*

A hole broken through a wall. Cool air. Screaming and sirens.

And anger, so much anger.

Then nothing.

The hospital room was blinding white. Betty was hooked up to tubes and life-support machines, unconscious. She looked so small.

A strong hand landed on his shoulder. He looked up to see General Ross staring at him. You've got a lot of nerve coming in here after what you did, *General Ross said.*

Bruce had never felt so tired in his life, so filled with misery. Worst of all was the rage that lingered in his blood. He could feel it, waiting for its chance to escape again. The monster wanted out, and he didn't know how long he could hold it back.

I just wanted to see her, *he said.* Make sure she's all right.

She'll be all right as soon as you leave her alone, *General* ·

Ross said. Permanently. Steer clear of her. You're a project asset now. That's all.

He felt his pulse start to race, and knew the monster was waking up again. Terrified, he pushed past General Ross and ran—out of the hospital, out of the country, out of Betty's life. He didn't stop running.

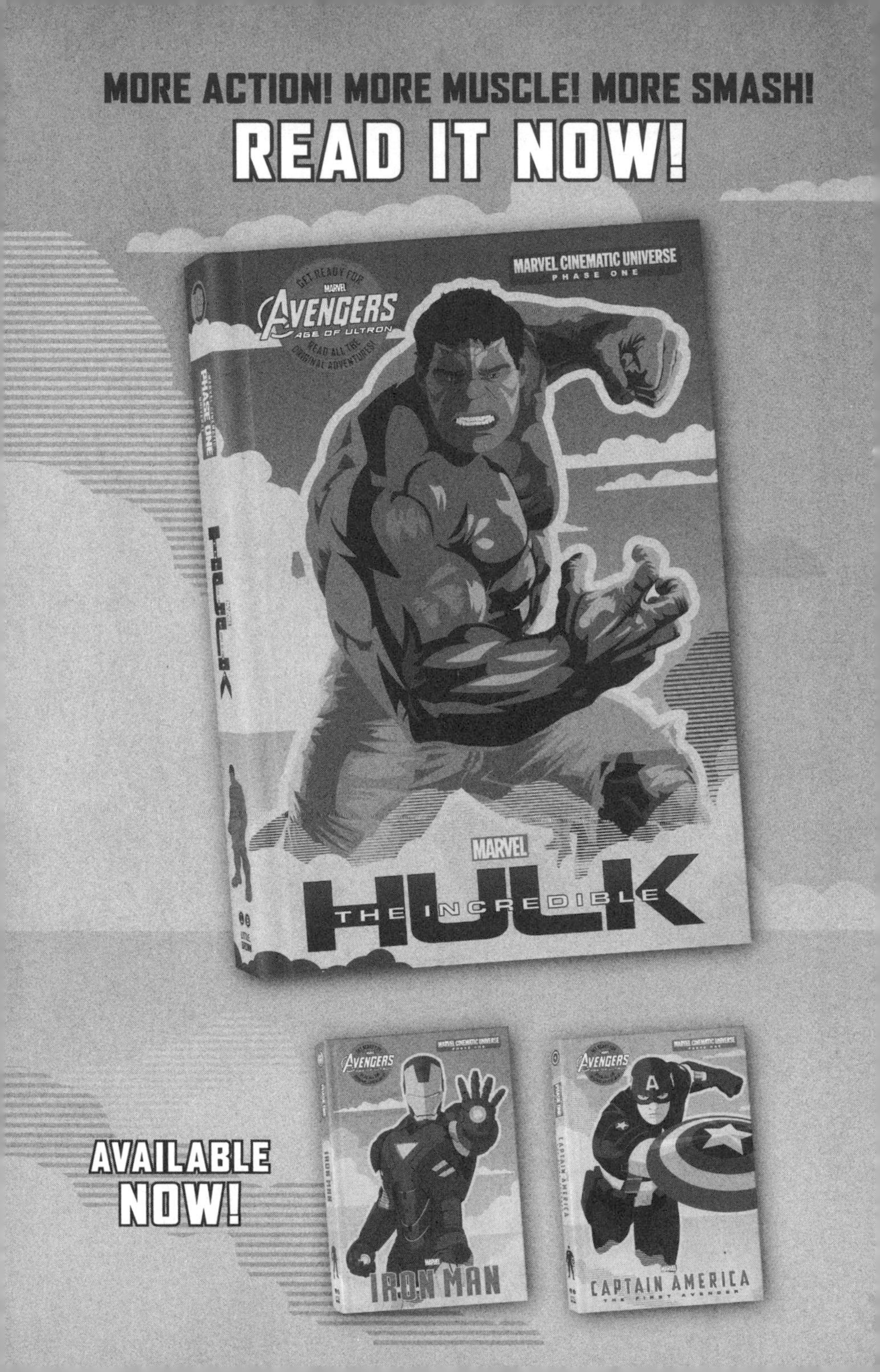

MORE ACTION! MORE MUSCLE! MORE SMASH!
READ IT NOW!
GET READY FOR
MARVEL
AVENGERS
AGE OF ULTRON
READ ALL THE ORIGINAL ADVENTURES!
MARVEL CINEMATIC UNIVERSE
PHASE ONE
MARVEL
THE INCREDIBLE HULK
AVAILABLE NOW!
MARVEL CINEMATIC UNIVERSE
PHASE ONE
IRON MAN
MARVEL CINEMATIC UNIVERSE
PHASE ONE
CAPTAIN AMERICA
THE FIRST AVENGER